David Marsh has co-authored several published non-fiction books about Leeds. He also authored a short story entitled *Billy* which was included in the anthology *Shorts From West Yorkshire*. His interests are writing, playing guitar and amateur dramatics. David is married and lives in West Yorkshire.

Flesh and Blood

David Marsh

Flesh and Blood

Vanguard Press

VANGUARD PAPERBACK

© Copyright 2023
David Marsh

The right of David Marsh to be identified as author of
this work has been asserted by him in accordance with the
Copyright, Designs and Patents Act 1988.

All Rights Reserved

No reproduction, copy or transmission of this publication
may be made without written permission.
No paragraph of this publication may be reproduced,
copied or transmitted save with the written permission of the publisher,
or in accordance with the provisions
of the Copyright Act 1956 (as amended).

Any person who commits any unauthorised act in relation to
this publication may be liable to criminal
prosecution and civil claims for damages.

A CIP catalogue record for this title is
available from the British Library.

ISBN 978 1 83794 095 0

Vanguard Press is an imprint of
Pegasus Elliot Mackenzie Publishers Ltd.
www.pegasuspublishers.com

This is a work of fiction. Names, characters, businesses, places, events and
incidents are either the product of the author's imagination or used in a fictitious
manner. Any resemblance to actual persons, living or dead, or actual events is
purely coincidental.

First Published in 2023

Vanguard Press
Sheraton House Castle Park
Cambridge England

Printed & Bound in Great Britain

For Sarah, Poppy and Bobby

Thanks to everyone who took the time to read and comment on the various drafts of this book. It is very much appreciated.

1

Lauren caught the man looking at her for the second time. The train had only just left Leeds and as she relaxed in her seat trying to shake off a long, tiring day, she noticed a rugged, somewhat watery-eyed man glancing across at her. He was trying to hide the fact of course, but he wasn't discreet enough. Lauren's eye was too quick. She guessed he must be somewhere in his mid-fifties and couldn't recall ever having seen him before on her commute home. Their eyes met for the briefest of moments. She saw a kind of sorrow in his expression, as if he were somehow burdened by something, but why he should be looking over at her in particular she could only guess. It was possible she'd met the man at the university library where she worked, maybe he was an academic; however, unless someone particularly stood out from the crowd she didn't remember faces, well, not academic ones at any rate. Perhaps though, he remembered hers. She wasn't concerned so she fished her phone out of her jeans as the middle-aged man now turned his attention to what was going on outside the window. She quickly punched a text to her gran saying she'd be home in half an hour before browsing the internet. Her fingers danced nimbly over the screen, backtracking here and there when something caught her interest. She took a deep breath and tugged at her tee shirt collar to cool herself down. July was proving to be hot, and it was a constant battle on public transport trying to keep comfortable in the stifling atmosphere. She scrabbled in her bag for her compact and flicked it open. Lauren didn't wear much make-up, just a touch of mascara and a very pale pink lipstick when she could be bothered. She adjusted her hair. She liked it with its extra length, something that had been forced on her during the Covid lockdown and how it fell loosely onto her shoulders, the parting just off centre. She dabbed mascara onto her long lashes, made a few faces as she appraised her work and snapped the compact closed. Now at least she didn't look like she'd been dragged through a hedge. She went back to her phone. Josh had sent her a message. Apparently he'd got some news to tell her. They hadn't been going out for very long (eight weeks and three days according to Lauren's calculations — early signs of triumph for internet dating) and were still very much consumed by lust. They always tried to meet up on a Wednesday evening as it made the wait for the weekend a bit more bearable when they could spend longer together. As she replied to his text, she glanced over to the adjacent seat and noticed that the middle-aged man was looking at her again. As had happened before, the moment she caught his gaze, he turned his head and looked out of the window. She still didn't think much of it — he seemed a harmless sort, it wasn't as if she didn't occasionally gawp at folk herself, besides, the train was busy, and you had to look somewhere.

Lauren didn't like Fitzwilliam station very much. It was too small; the ticket machine never worked; there were too many steps up to the car park and the platform shelters were always vandalised. The only good thing about Fitzy was that it had a great rail service to and from Leeds. She stepped wearily off the train and headed through the press of people up to the car park. To her frustration, she found that a car was obstructing her own. This was a habit of drivers who had come to pick up friends or family from the station and couldn't be bothered to park in a designated area. Lauren offloaded her bag and got into her car, hoping this would be a sufficient hint to the waiting driver blocking her way to move on. No such luck. She flashed her lights and blasted the horn before the penny dropped. The offending car dutifully moved out of the way.

"At last!" Lauren said to herself as she eased out of her space and onto the main road. She checked the rear-view mirror and caught sight of the middle-aged man once again, his phone in the air apparently pointed in her direction, though she couldn't be absolutely certain. Perhaps she was reading more into things than was there. Frowning slightly, she slipped the car into second gear and headed for home.

Once Lauren had washed the day away, put on some fresh clothes and wolfed down the tuna salad her gran had made, she helped load the dishwasher before announcing she was going over to see Josh.

"You're seeing a lot of this boy, Lauren," her gran said lightly. "I don't know why you don't bring him round home a bit more often. Anyone would think you were embarrassed of us; you hardly ever ask him in."

Lauren was already reaching for the door with one arm and grabbing her jacket from the hook with the other. She pecked her gran on the cheek.

"Don't be silly. Besides, you're usually in bed when I get home."

"Text me when you arrive," her gran fussed as Lauren finally got out of the door.

"Don't I always?" She heard this request every time she went out of an evening. Living with your fussy maternal grandparents could be a bit stifling at times, especially when you were rapidly approaching twenty, but it was all she knew. Her mum had died of a brain haemorrhage when Lauren was only two, and her dad had died tragically in a car accident a month before she was born. Being officially adopted by them seemed to reignite their parental instincts to such an extent that they didn't always know when to cut Lauren some slack. Twenty-first century parenting was somewhat different to the eighties, however, for the most part, they were doing just fine.

"Say 'hi' to Grandad for me when he gets home." She got into her car and headed off, sounding the horn as her gran waved from the doorstep.

The Duck and Drake was one of their favourite haunts. It was popular with young adults although this evening it was quiet, even by mid-week standards. Lauren could see that Josh wasn't his usual self as he sat hunched over his beer.

"Are you all right?" she asked him, catching a whiff of his scent. She liked it. Arabia she remembered it was called. Its strong, musky fragrance was richly exotic. It was expensive too. She'd looked it up on Amazon thinking it would be a nice Christmas or birthday gift for him. The cheapest she could get it for was eighty pounds. It was certainly on the top side of her budget, but Christmas was still a way off and he'd had his birthday a month before they'd started going out. She had plenty of time to save up. He was a smart lad who liked his checked shirts and slim-fitting trousers. His wiry hair was well trimmed, and he was always clean-shaven. This evening was no exception, but his usually dazzling eyes were no longer sparkling like the sapphires that she loved so much.

Josh shrugged. "There's a bit of shit going on at home that's all."

"Arguing with your mum and dad again?"

"Something like that." He drew a finger around the rim of his beer glass. "I hate them sometimes," he said.

"All parents can be annoying at times," Lauren said, trying to soften him a bit.

"There's annoying and then there's my mum and dad. I tell you, if there's such thing as reincarnation, I don't want to be born to those two again. I sometimes wish I was like you."

"Like me?"

"You know. Adopted."

Lauren frowned. It was a strange thing to say.

"At least you know your mum and dad, which is more than I ever did. Besides, being adopted by your grandparents doesn't count. They're still family. So what were you rowing about?"

Josh produced two slightly crumpled pieces of paper from his pocket and placed them on the table. He smoothed them out and pushed them towards Lauren.

"This," he said.

"Wow," Lauren said as she clocked the spacious, fully furnished apartment. "Are you thinking of renting this?" She sipped her lime and soda. "Eight hundred a month! I didn't know mechanics earned so much."

Josh shrugged. "They don't, but I've got some savings and I reckon I could manage. Which is more than Mum and Dad think."

"I'd no idea you were even thinking of moving out."

"It's been brewing for ages. Home life's doing my head in."

"Your mum and dad aren't that bad. They seemed nice enough to me."

"It's me they're not nice with. They think I should save to buy a place and not chuck money away on rent."

"They're just trying to help."

"I'm twenty-two, Lauren, I can make up my own mind about things. They're always interfering, or trying to take control, like I'm incapable of doing anything for myself."

Lauren turned her attention back to the apartment. "It's lovely, Josh, it really is. Look at the kitchen! It's massive."

16

"Yeah, the bedrooms aren't bad either!" Josh was bright all of a sudden. "Plus it would give us a bit of privacy."

He winked and Lauren felt her cheeks run hot.

"You're not doing this for *us* are you?" She was sure her face was on fire.

"No," Josh said defensively. "I just thought you might be interested that's all. Anyway, what's wrong with thinking a little about the future?"

"I'm sorry, of course I'm interested, I didn't mean to—"

Josh snatched the papers from Lauren and stuffed them into his pocket.

"Forget it; you're as bad as Mum and Dad." He took a swig of his lager. "It's just something I'm thinking about."

Lauren bit her lip. This was a habit of hers whenever she was unsure how to respond to a situation. She wanted to say something but saw that Josh's expression was one of indignant petulance, so she decided to keep quiet. With the relationship still so young she didn't want to risk spoiling things before they'd got properly going. The ensuing silence was uncomfortable, like the stillness before a storm only the first rumbles of thunder had already sounded, and she didn't like them one little bit. This was the first time there had been any hint of friction between them since they'd been going out. Lauren prided herself on how they both got along, much to the envy of her friends at work.

"You want another?" Josh asked rising from his seat.

"No, thank you," Lauren said somewhat withdrawn. Josh went over to the bar and got himself another pint. When he returned his mood seemed brighter.

"There's a good local band down here on Saturday if you're interested. Starts quite early though. Seven o'clock."

Lauren still felt bruised.

"If that's what you want to do," she said stiffly.

Josh flashed a toothy grin.

"Yeah," he said. "It is."

2

Lauren was quiet at work the next day, which was unusual for her. Her best friend, Pritvia Dhawan, a down-to-earth, slim girl originally from Bangalore, who brightened every day by wearing the most vivid coloured dresses she could get her hands on, managed to tease Lauren into opening up as they lunched together in the nearby park. Whenever the weather was half decent they always got some fresh air and a change of scenery, generally perching on the same bench that gave the best view of the park. The somewhat sanitised academic surroundings of the library could get a bit oppressive at times.

"So are you going to tell me what's on your mind or are you going to keep scaring the customers away?" Pritvia pushed her large glasses onto the bridge of her nose. They had a habit of slipping down.

"I'm not that bad am I?" Lauren said, sounding a little surprised.

"I've seen happier faces on *Eastenders*."

Lauren sighed and came clean. There was little point in fobbing her friend off. Pritvia was as sharp as a razor and had little truck with people who wallowed in self-pity. Often brusque, she always managed to get to the heart of the matter, a quality that Lauren found both endearing and annoying.

"Josh was in a bit of a mood last night."

"I thought you two were really hitting it off."

"We are. It's just that he doesn't really get along with his mum and dad and he'd had a bit of a row with them before we went out, and then I managed to upset him, but it was over something or nothing really." She went on to explain about the apartment and that she hoped he wasn't looking for a place for her sake.

"So you guys had a bit of a barney?" Pritvia found it amusing.

"I wouldn't call it *that* exactly. He got a bit touchy about what I'd said that's all."

"But you're still together, right?"

"Yes," Lauren nodded.

"And you kissed and made up?"

Another nod.

"So where's your problem?"

Lauren shrugged. "I don't know. He's usually so easy-going."

"Maybe you disappointed him a bit," Pritvia reasoned. "You pissed on his bonfire. That and the fact he was equally pissed at his mum and dad."

"I was thinking about it all last night. I didn't get a wink."

"So what will you say if he mentions getting his own place again?"

"I don't know. I just want to go out and have a good time. I don't want to think about anything serious."

"Doesn't going back to a luxury apartment qualify as a having good time?"

"It all seems a bit too fast, that's all I'm saying. Sex is one thing, but…"

"Oh, Lauren you can be so old-fashioned at times," Pritvia said, the amused expression still on her face. "I suppose you get it from living with your grandparents — no offence. And to be honest, they're positively Jurassic judging by what you tell me. I mean where did they spend the 1970s, in a bomb shelter or something?"

"No they didn't!" Lauren said indignantly.

Pritvia sensed that she might have pushed things a bit too far.

"What I'm saying is, you're quite happy to shag him but the moment he talks about getting a place of his own you get all stuffy. What if he'd already got his own pad before you met him? You'd never be away from the place."

"That would be different," Lauren said. "I could just *sense* something that's all."

"Like what?"

Lauren shrugged. "It was just a feeling I got, like he's maybe pushing things?"

"He just wants a place of his own, Lauren. There's nothing unusual in that. Don't read so much into it. Anyway, I'm looking forward to meeting him at your birthday bash, I'll see if he's worth all the fuss."

Yes, her birthday bash wasn't so far away now, she'd virtually got everything organised. A week next Sunday she'd be the big two-oh. Her teenage days gone forever.

"Make sure you keep your paws off him," Lauren said. "I know what a flirt you can be."

Pritvia grinned. "*Moi!* Never!"

The commute home was as busy as ever. Lauren's mood brightened considerably as she read Josh's latest message, which had just pinged through saying how much he was looking forward to the weekend. She responded in kind, feeling the world was an altogether better place all of a sudden. She realised that she'd been brooding unnecessarily and as Pritvia had pointed out, it wasn't as if the two of them hadn't made up or left on good terms. She supposed she was a bit disappointed in herself, of her own reaction to his plans, and in her expectations of Josh. As she relaxed and slunk into her seat, she whiled away the journey scrolling through her phone. Its triviality was just what she needed after a day of pointless chewing over negative thoughts. As she'd done on the previous day, she glanced towards the seat adjacent to hers. This wasn't anything premeditated; it was simply a reflex action. She instantly recognised the man who'd been observing her yesterday. She thought she'd caught him looking at her again and pretended to rummage in her bag for something, discreetly flicking her eyes towards the man, but now his attention appeared elsewhere. When the train pulled in to Fitzwilliam, the man was already waiting by the exit doors of the carriage. As the conductor released the doors, the man turned to Lauren and motioned for her to go first. She hadn't expected such chivalry and uttered a meek "Thank you", before stepping off the train. When she reached her car the man was nowhere in sight.

Saturday night was slow in arriving. Lauren had been looking forward to going out all day and couldn't wait to see Josh and hear the band. She knew the pub would be heaving so she'd opted for a casual look, a tee shirt and best jeans. The day had been hot and sunny, and she didn't fancy wearing one of her summer dresses for the gig, especially since someone had managed to spill some red wine over her the last time they'd seen a band at the venue. Her tee shirt could take it, her dresses couldn't. Josh was wearing another of his checked shirts coupled with dark trousers. He didn't seem to be a jeans person. They walked hand in hand to the pub, their conversation light and easy. Lauren noticed that he was wearing a different scent this evening.

"Obsidian," he said. "A birthday present from my grandparents. I'm not too sure about it myself."

"It's nice," Lauren said brightly. She hoped that he might say something about her fragrance, California, as she'd bought it especially for tonight, but he said nothing.

They went straight over to the bar. It was quite congested and already bordering on the raucous. The band had set up on the small stage but wouldn't be performing for another hour. Josh nodded to a few people he knew. He bought himself a lager and pulled a face when Lauren said she'd have a lime and soda.

"You should think about taking a taxi home sometimes. You don't always have to drive. Live a little."

"I don't mind," Lauren said defensively.

Josh handed over her drink. "There's a table over there; if we're quick, we can just make it before someone nips in."

The conversation remained easy, and Lauren felt that she had finally put to rest the ghost of Wednesday evening. It was clear that Josh hadn't been arguing with anyone today.

"Gran was wondering whether you'd like to come over again sometime soon," she said feeling relieved that Josh was his usual self. "She's complaining she doesn't get to see much of you."

Josh sipped his lager. "Made an impression have I?"

"You must have."

"It's not going to be a big deal or anything, is it?"

"What do you mean?"

"A buffet lunch and the works."

Lauren laughed. "I don't know. Anyway, what would be wrong with that?"

"My ex's mum gave me the full works once. It was seafood paella, full of squid and garlic prawns. Bloody horrible it was. I nearly choked on every mouthful."

Lauren flinched as he mentioned his ex. She knew she wasn't Josh's first girlfriend, but nevertheless, hearing about girls from the past didn't sit comfortably with her.

"Gran wouldn't make anything like that. Grandad would hate it."

Josh shrugged. "I suppose it wouldn't do any harm to regale them with my charm and wit."

Lauren beamed at him and rubbed his leg affectionately with her own. "They like you Josh. I think they're pleased I've finally found someone decent."

"You've had a few rough ones, eh?"

Lauren shrugged. They hadn't really talked about past partners until now and Lauren's wounds were a bit raw.

"Well, not rough, no," she said after a moment. "Phil decided he wanted his freedom, as if I was controlling him or something! And Adie went off with Michelle Carter." She almost spat Michelle's name. "It didn't do my self-esteem any good." This was an understatement. Lauren's confidence had in fact taken a sever knock over the matter, and it had taken months for her to recover. Once she felt like her old self again, she decided that online dating might have better results. Josh was her first compatible match.

"Still hurts does it?"

"We used to be good friends, me and Michelle." Lauren sipped her drink. "I sometimes think she stole Adie to get back at me."

"Get back at you?"

"It goes back to when we were at school. I wrongly accused her of stealing my pencil set and she never forgave me for it. I've lost count of how many times I apologised to her but the damage had been done. I'm a bit more careful of what I say nowadays. I really liked her."

"How can you accuse one of your mates of nicking your pencils?"

Lauren shrugged. "I let her borrow them one day and they went missing. Then I saw them in her bag a few days later, put two and two together and made eight. It turned out that Brian Reeves had taken them and then put them in there, so she'd get the blame, which she did. As if that wasn't bad enough, he'd chewed all the ends. Gran told me off about it for not being more careful."

Josh allowed himself a little laugh. "Well I don't fancy chewing any pencils, and I'm not going to run off with your ex-mate. And for what it's worth, I like your gran and grandad too, they're all right they are, even if they're a bit old-fashioned."

"There's nothing wrong with Gran and Grandad," Lauren said, clearly on the defensive. "Why does everybody think they're from the Ark or something?"

"Hey, hey, keep your hair on, I didn't mean anything by it," Josh said, backing down. "Anyway, if your grandparents are from the Ark, Mum and Dad are before time itself. You look like a younger version of your gran, you know that?"

Lauren lowered her hackles and let Josh's earlier remark go.

"Gran says I'm like my mum. I've got her eyes."

"Yeah, I was thinking the other day that it must be a bit strange for you, not having a mum or dad."

"Gran and Grandad are my mum and dad," Lauren said simply.

"Do you wonder much about your mum and dad? I know I would in your shoes."

"Sometimes. I know that dad was a bit of a womaniser and he had quite a few affairs. I don't know whether Mum was blind to his faults or whether she just accepted him the way he was, but Gran and Grandad don't talk about him much, and when they do it always sounds a bit caustic. I stopped asking about him a long time ago. The only photo I've got of him is the official one they had taken on their wedding day."

"So what actually happened to your dad?"

Lauren shrugged. "All I know is that he was killed in a car crash down south somewhere. He'd been visiting his mum."

"If you want to know more about him, why don't you ask her then? She's your grandma after all."

Lauren shook her head. "She died when I was three," she said. "And I never saw my other grandad because he died a few years before I was born."

"Christ, sounds like your dad's family were a bit jinxed."

"You're like your dad," Lauren said, shifting the conversation onto Josh's family now. "You've got his nose."

"Yeah, it's a bit of a hooter," Josh laughed. "It's the main insignia on the family coat of arms." He took a massive swig of his beer and belched which lightened things much to Lauren's relief, and it set the tone for the rest of the evening. The contrast to Wednesday night couldn't have been starker and once the band started, the atmosphere became electric. Josh was drinking heavily and was becoming increasingly boisterous. He could certainly knock it back, Lauren observed. As the venue got more crowded they eventually abandoned their table to get closer to the stage. The band was playing something by Snow Patrol; it was an old number that seemed to be going down well. Although Lauren was stone cold sober, she was giddy on the atmosphere just the same. As she swayed her body to the music, she felt a tap on her shoulder.

"Zak!" she said, turning and throwing her arms around the new arrival, then planting a kiss on his cheek. She could smell his sweat as well as the beer on his breath. "I thought you were in London. Why didn't you say you were coming up to visit? " She had to shout to make herself heard.

"Short notice," he said, craning his neck to shout down Lauren's ear over the noise. "I would have messaged but you know how it is when you've got a thousand things going off at once."

"Yes," Lauren said, thrilled to have met up with her friend again. She grabbed Josh's attention and introduced him to Zak.

"This is Zak," she said. "He's an old friend."

Josh looked a bit wary but shook Zak's proffered hand, nevertheless.

"You two go back a long way then do you?" he said, moving away from the stage.

"I used to live a few doors down," Zak said, running a hand through his bristly hair.

"Best friends for a while," Lauren added with mock indignation. "Then he took himself off to London to work in a private gallery. How long are you staying around?"

"A few weeks. Gives me a chance to catch up with my past."

"Have you got a lot of past to catch up with?" Josh asked, cockily.

"A fair bit."

Lauren was pleased. "You'll be around for my birthday! I'm having a party next Sunday; you'll have to come. Gran and Grandad would love to see you again." Zak had been a regular visitor to Lauren's as they'd grown up. He was a couple of years older than her but that hadn't affected their friendship, even through their early teens, when thrashing hormones started to wreak havoc with their emotions and brains. Everyone who knew them thought that they were a couple, but their relationship was more reflective of close siblings. Lauren had hoped that things might develop a bit further, but when Zak had the opportunity to move to London through his numerous family connections, he'd jumped at the chance, much to Lauren's disappointment. Now they mainly kept in touch through social media, although she did manage to visit him occasionally for the odd weekend.

Zak nodded. "Sounds cool."

"Great!" Lauren said. "I'll message you the details nearer the time."

Josh turned back to the stage as Lauren and Zak continued to catch up on old times, the warmth of their friendship was not lost on him. He looked at his watch. It was well past midnight, and no one was leaving. It was time for another drink.

It wasn't a long walk from the pub back to Josh's house. The evening had been better than Lauren had hoped. Her ears were still ringing from the loud music, but she didn't care. She chatted happily to Josh until they reached the front gate of his house. She turned and faced him and kissed him on the lips, but it was like kissing a corpse.

"I think you've had too much to drink," Lauren giggled.

"Maybe."

She kissed him again, but his lack of passion was palpable. "Are you all right?"

He eased Lauren's arms from around his waist. "I don't like being disrespected," he said, his expression almost glacial.

"What?"

"C'mon, don't pretend you don't know."

Lauren didn't know.

"I don't understand. What are you talking about?"

"You want me to spell it out?"

Lauren frowned.

"I'm not playing shit to *his* piss," Josh said.

"You're talking about Zak?"

"Course I'm talking about Zak. Just how good a friend is he to you?"

Lauren could feel her heart start to thump as it dawned on her what Josh was suggesting.

"He's a friend, that's all." She tried to soothe him, but he shrugged her off. "Josh, you've got it all wrong." The evening was rapidly turning sour.

"I hope I have, Lauren. I'm not going to be messed about."

"You're not being messed about."

He could see that Lauren's eyes were a little moist. "Look, it's late, maybe I've had a bit too much to drink. I need to get my head down. I'll call you tomorrow, yeah?"

Lauren said nothing.

Josh kissed her lightly on the lips and went through the gate. He turned to wave to her, but she'd already climbed into her car. He heard her start the engine and drive off.

3

Josh was late getting up. He wasn't the earliest of risers on a Sunday at the best of times, but today his head was as thick as a Victorian fog. The only thing he could stomach was a black coffee and some toast that he'd almost cremated. He was on his own in the house; his parents had gone off for the day visiting friends up in Durham. They'd be late back. It suited Josh; he wasn't in the mood for company. He freshened himself up and decided he'd get some of the summer air. He grabbed his phone and checked it for messages. He'd eight in all, none from Lauren.

It was a bright day, the warmth of the afternoon sun on his back made him feel human again. He was still annoyed with Lauren though; no sunshine was going to fix that. He replayed last night in his head as he made his way down the street, crossing the road and heading for a narrow bridle path that led out towards some open countryside. He'd walked with Lauren on this path not so long ago and it conjured pleasant memories, although today they were bittersweet. Everything had been going fine last night until that little shit had turned up. From that point on he had been second best. He perched on a makeshift bench fashioned out of a large tree stump and opened up his phone. He found

Lauren's Facebook page, clicked on her profile and then the list of her friends. It didn't take him long to find Zak. The lad's cherubic smile and straw-coloured hair were unmistakable. He checked Zak's relationship status. He was single.

He called Lauren just after five. She didn't pick up. Whether she was away from her phone or was ignoring him he didn't know, but it only added to his frustration. He knew she occasionally went out with her grandparents on a Sunday; they were always getting invited to places or visiting local beauty spots, but she hadn't mentioned anything yesterday. Perhaps she'd gone shopping with some of her friends. Maybe she was with Zak. It would make sense considering how friendly they'd been last night. A pendulous cloud descended on his already tight mood. He could feel anger as well as frustration surging through his veins. He cursed and called Lauren again. Her phone rang out but still she didn't respond.

"C'mon, answer," he urged. He allowed the phone to ring until her voicemail kicked in. He didn't bother leaving a message. He preferred a more direct approach.

In less than twenty minutes he was driving down to Lauren's. The houses down Lakeland Walk where she lived were all neat and of a kind, typical of the late 1990s. Detached, with open plan gardens and spacious driveways harbouring BMWs and Audis, the folk around here weren't short of a bob or two. Josh was interested in only one car though, and that was Lauren's blue Corsa. There was a white BMW five series parked directly in front of the garage and a new red Mini that suggested her grandparents were at home, which was more than could be said of Lauren. He pulled up and considered what to do. Should he wait for her until she arrived home, or knock on the door and ask for her? He couldn't stand not knowing where she was or whom she was with. If she was with Zak, he wasn't sure what he would do. He swore and thumped the steering wheel. His mind refused to settle, images whirled around his head of Lauren and Zak together and he couldn't get them out of his head. Unable to contain his frustration any longer, he got out of his car, marched determinedly up to the front door and rapped hard on the knocker. He noticed a sign on the letterbox that hadn't been there the last time he'd visited. It read: *'No cold callers or junk mail'*. It seemed to take an age before Lauren's grandad finally opened the door.

"Hi," Josh said as casually as he could muster. "I was just passing by and wondered if I could wait for Lauren, if she's not going to be too long." He had no idea whether Lauren had mentioned anything about their awkward parting last night though the look on her grandad's face suggested only warmth, so he supposed he was in the clear.

"Come in lad," he said stepping aside and hurriedly tucked his tee shirt into his trousers while bravely pulling in his paunch at the same time. "She shouldn't be too long now."

Josh could hear the rattle of cutlery and drawers being opened in the kitchen as he was ushered through into the spacious living room. Lauren's grandad motioned for Josh to take a seat. "We hadn't arranged anything definite for today," Josh said as he eased onto the sofa, "but I wanted to see her. I've tried calling her mobile, but she isn't answering."

Lauren's grandad shrugged. "She's out with some friends from work, shopping I think she said."

Josh was relieved that he hadn't mentioned Zak's name. Before he had a chance to ask any more questions, Lauren's grandma came in.

"Hello Josh," she said brightly. "Lovely to see you. Lauren's running a bit late; you hadn't arranged something with her had you?"

Josh shook his head and reaffirmed what he's already told Lauren's grandad. "I just called in on the off chance, Iris."

"I'd only been saying to Geoff this morning that we should see a bit more of you," Iris said.

Geoff nodded.

"Would you like a drink, lad? Beer?"

Josh shook his head. The thought of alcohol made him shudder. His head, not to mention his stomach was still out of kilter.

"I'll have a black coffee if that's okay."

Iris immediately went to make the brew. Josh and Geoff passed trivial conversation until the coffee arrived along with a plateful of biscuits. Iris seemed to be making an extra effort in Josh's presence, combing her hand through her fine, grey hair, and straightening the hem of her flowing summer dress.

She's good for her age, Josh thought. There was something almost regal about her, how she held herself as she moved about the place. In Josh's experience, tall people had a tendency to walk with slightly hunched shoulders but not Iris, nor Lauren for that matter. They both had poise. Geoff, on the other hand, was a somewhat dumpy, squat sort of bloke. He was a good few inches shorter than his wife but that didn't mean he was lacking in his own self-assurance or that his gait was in any way slovenly. He seemed happy in his own skin, made no pretence about his potbelly and was allowing his grey hair to gain a complete stranglehold on his once dark mane. Josh had seen so many middle-aged and elderly men make a complete arse of their hair, messing with various shades of brown that generally came out the same shade as a dog turd — his own dad was a prime example of that. Geoff had more sense.

"Help yourself to a biscuit," Iris said, sitting in an armchair and crossing her legs.

Out of politeness Josh took one, hoping his still queasy stomach would hold the thing down. He nibbled it somewhat hesitantly and then took a swig of coffee. So far so good. He looked at his phone to see if Lauren had messaged him but there was nothing. Josh was glad that Iris had plenty of conversation in her, it meant that he could easily respond and go with the flow of things, but all the time he was anxiously waiting for Lauren. He weathered the niceties of convention for a further ten minutes before he heard the sound of a car pulling into the driveway. A quick glance through the window told him that finally Lauren was home. He could feel his heart quicken its beat as he heard Lauren clump into the hallway, dump her bags and hang her keys on a hook. A few moments later she came in, said "Hiya," and shot Josh a reproachful look, before perching on the sofa, being mindful to leave a gap between them both. She pointedly crossed her legs away from him.

"We were expecting you a bit sooner," Iris said. "Have you had a good time?"

"Yes," Lauren said.

"Hammering the old credit card, eh?" Josh said, his tone bright and cheerful.

"I bought a few things," Lauren said coolly.

Iris cut in. "Would you like to stay for some tea, Josh? It won't be much I'm afraid, but you'd be most welcome."

"No thanks," Josh said. "I'd just like to spend half an hour with Lauren and then I'll get off home, if that's all right."

He took Lauren's hand and said, "Shall we just have a turn around the block?"

Lauren shrugged. There was little point in making a scene; besides, she knew they would have to talk some time.

"I suppose," she said without enthusiasm and got up from the sofa.

"Don't rush back," Iris said. "There's nothing spoiling."

4

·

"Why did you come?" Lauren wanted to know as they headed down the street.

"Because you weren't answering your phone and I wanted to talk to you."

"Why would you want to talk to someone who disrespects you?" She sounded bitter.

"C'mon Lauren, I explained that. I had one too many."

"I thought we were getting on great. But now I'm not so sure. You were a funny road out last Wednesday, and last night you were horrible."

Josh took her by the hands and looked into her unforgiving eyes.

"All I can do is apologise. Let me make it up to you, please."

"I'm not treading on eggshells, Josh." She slipped out of his embrace and turned away.

"Well I don't intend to lay any eggs." He tugged gently at her arm, made her face him again.

"I mean it," Lauren said firmly.

"So do I." Josh's tone was soft with no trace of petulance. "Lauren, you're the best thing that's happened to me in a long time. I know I spoiled things a bit, it's just that… well… I don't want anything to get in the way that's all."

Lauren saw the sincerity in his eyes as his voice tailed off. She hated falling out with him, especially after they'd had such a good start. "All I want is for us to enjoy ourselves."

"And that's what I want too. I'll tell you what, let's go to the pictures tomorrow, and maybe a bite to eat afterwards. My treat."

"I can't tomorrow, I'm working late."

"Tuesday then. C'mon, Lauren." He was like a puppy pleading with her.

"As long as you promise not to drink," she said, thawing at last.

He smiled and pecked her on the forehead. "I'll be driving, I won't touch a drop."

"All right."

"That's my girl."

5

On Monday evening Lauren called in at the local Co-op on her way home to pick up some yoghurt and a couple of magazines. She'd meant to get them in Leeds, but she was late leaving work and had had to dash for the train. It wasn't busy so she knew she could be in and out in a flash. She didn't notice the middle-aged man until she was at the self-service checkout. He'd been buying some bread and didn't seem to be aware of her. She pushed her items through the scanner, stealing a glance to her left where the man was just bagging up his things. He didn't seem the least bit interested in her as she packed her yoghurt and magazines. Nothing about the man suggested anything sinister at all. She paid for her items and headed out. When she got to her car, she dumped her bags on the back seat and checked her phone. Josh had just sent her a message asking her to pick whichever film she fancied for tomorrow evening. He'd buy the tickets in advance. She fired a message back saying that she would as soon as she'd had something to eat.

As she eased out of the car park, she noticed the middle-aged man just leaving the store. He had his phone in his hand and it was raised at a peculiar angle, as if it were pointing towards her car. She drove steadily by and checked the rear-view mirror, making sure she could clearly see his reflection. It was difficult to tell what he was up to. Perhaps he was trying to get a decent signal, she mused, the reception wasn't always good in this area. She bit on her lip, unsure what to make of it and headed home.

6

The last thing that Lauren needed was a cancelled train. The 17:22 was usually reliable but not today. She'd have to catch the Pontefract train and then get back to Fitzwilliam for her car. Her gran was going to have to bail her out otherwise she wouldn't be home in time to meet Josh. To make matters worse, she could see the middle-aged man, phone clamped to his ear, probably having to make similar arrangements himself. She hadn't caught him looking at her today, but she wanted to avoid him all the same. She called her gran and explained the situation. Yes, she'd pick her up. Lauren then messaged Josh; it was going to be tight to meet him for seven, could he make it half past? Yes. No problem.

The Pontefract train was packed, swelled by the Fitzwilliam travellers having to make the same journey as Lauren. It was stuffy and claustrophobic; everyone seemed tired but luckily she managed to find a seat. She'd lost sight of the middle-aged man and hoped he was on another carriage or better still, a different train altogether. Her eyelids felt heavy, and she almost nodded off two or three times, but she managed to fight off the urge to succumb, knowing if she did, even for ten minutes, she'd feel the worse for it.

When the train finally arrived, she scanned the unfamiliar car park for her gran's Mini. She eventually picked it out and moved lugubriously over and almost fell into the passenger seat.

"You look shattered, love. Are you sure you want to go out tonight?" her gran said as she started to thread her way out through the swarming herd of cars and commuters.

"I'm all right," Lauren said. "Besides, it's too late to change things now and Josh has already got the tickets."

A silver Volkswagen came alongside, driven by an attractive blonde-haired woman. Beside her in the passenger seat Lauren recognised the middle-aged man. *Hmm, so he's married, or has a partner at least,* she mused, already beginning to play with her phone.

"I told you I saw Zak the other day didn't I?" Lauren said, scrolling through various screens.

"Yes. It's a shame about you and him."

"Shame? In what way?"

"Well, you were so close. We all liked Zak."

"Things change."

The Volkswagen overtook. Lauren watched as it picked up speed and headed down towards the junction ahead.

"The forecast is nice for Sunday," Iris said. "We'll be able to use the garden for your party."

"Sounds good," Lauren said, continuing to scroll through her phone.

"Do you ever put that thing down?"

"I like to know what's going on."

"There's more to life than being glued to your phone."

Lauren sighed and stuffed her phone into her bag.

"It'll be nice to see Zak again," Iris said, picking up speed. "I take it you've asked him to your party."

"Yes," Lauren said. "I've asked him."

7

She'd chosen the latest Thor movie thinking it would suit Josh. It wasn't her particular taste in films, but she quite fancied Chris Hemsworth so she knew she could make the best of it. Lauren hoped the noise and action sequences might keep her awake, as she still felt tired. When they finally settled into their seats, she snuggled against Josh who arched an affectionate arm around her. Despite her best intentions, she was asleep within ten minutes.

The film was three quarters of the way through when she awoke. She hadn't the foggiest idea of what was going on, but Josh seemed to be enjoying it. She looked at her watch. It was ten o'clock already and she was famished. Hopefully they'd manage to grab a bite before it got too late. When the film finally finished, Josh suggested they tried the steak bar just around the corner. It was quite a pricey place, but Josh insisted that he paid. They sat on high chairs by the windows. Josh ordered the food. He chose a steak burger. Lauren decided to have a chicken kebab. Neither was drinking alcohol. Lauren said she'd have her usual lime and soda and Josh tried the non-alcoholic lager. When it arrived he took a sip and pulled a face.

"It's like bloody screen wash," he complained. "No wonder people stick with the booze."

Lauren giggled. "I didn't know you'd drunk screen wash before."

"I haven't," Josh laughed. "But if I did, this is what it would taste like."

The food arrived served by a girl who didn't look old enough to be up this late. Lauren and Josh dug wolfishly into their food.

"Don't forget that my party starts at one on Sunday," Lauren said, sliding a chunk of chicken from the skewer.

"Even though it's in my honour, I'll have to help out a bit, so don't think I'll be ignoring you."

Josh chewed on his burger and sipped his screen wash.

"Why would I think that?" he said.

"Zak will be there," Lauren said a little hesitantly, watching Josh's reaction carefully.

Josh shrugged with an air of nonchalance. "It's your gig."

"You don't mind then?"

Josh didn't immediately respond and Lauren worried that he might say something about the last time they'd met. "No," he said at last. "I don't mind."

Lauren wasn't sure that he meant it judging by the taut expression on his face, but his answer was good enough.

8

T he middle-aged man made sure he sat directly behind Lauren. He'd watched her arrive at the station, pass through the gates and make for platform 10B. He'd got used to tracking her now and how to keep out of her eyeshot. He knew where she generally liked to sit, it was easy to hover, wait for her to choose her seat and then settle somewhere close. Today was no exception. She was talking on her phone, and he could clearly hear a male voice on the other end. He leaned a little closer in, so close he could just detect the sweetness of her perfume. His ears were finely tuned into the conversation.

"Steady on, Josh, you're talking too fast."

"I said it's a nice place, I'm checking it out tonight; will you come with me?"

"What time are you going round?"

"I said half-six, but I can make it seven if it's easier. C'mon Lauren, this is important to me."

"I was supposed to be washing my hair tonight."

"Wash it tomorrow night. I'll pick you up at about quarter to seven, yeah?"

Lauren sighed. "All right," she said. It had been a long day and she was too tired to argue.

"Thanks. I think you'll like the place."

"It's you who has to like it, Josh."

"Yeah, but it'll be nice to get your approval."

As the conversation drifted into trivia, the man settled back in his chair and smiled to himself.

9

"Josh, it's a mausoleum; you'll die of old age inside a month!" Lauren said. "It smells of old people."

"It's not that bad, and it's a sight cheaper than that other place I showed you," Josh reasoned, disappointed that Lauren wasn't overly enamoured with the place.

It was an upper floor apartment of what had once been a Victorian mansion house. Long past its glory days, it was a shadow of its former self. Although it was fully furnished, it was nothing to write home about. The furniture itself was more of a menagerie of items bought at jumble sales and junk inherited from people's attics. Lauren peered into the kitchen and saw that it was in desperate need of modernising, although it was reasonably spacious.

"I don't know what your mum and dad will think," she said, wiping her hand across the worktop and examining it for dirt.

"Can't you try to sound a bit more enthusiastic?"

"There are better places than this, Josh."

"It's convenient for work, handy for town, and I can afford it."

Lauren said nothing and went into the bedroom. It was a good size, she'd give it that, but the whole building was drab.

"Are you so desperate to leave home that you'd live *here*?" she asked, looking at a crack on the ceiling.

"Desperate is an understatement."

Lauren went into the living room. Josh followed. The boards creaked under the worn carpet.

"I don't like it, Josh. You can do better." She could see the disappointment on his face. *Maybe I'm being a bit hard,* she thought. "But it's your choice."

"Yeah," Josh said. "It's my choice."

The next morning, Lauren was on reception duties early on, her mind a million miles from Josh and his apartment. She was focused on the steady stream of students needing access to the library. When her phone beeped that she had a text it couldn't have come at a worse time. (It was just after ten, when most students decided they could face the day.) The queue of customers was increasing by the minute and as the system had just crashed, were being temporarily held back, and despite Lauren's constant assurances that everything would soon be sorted, still caught a fair dollop of flak. She called for assistance, which was slow in coming. When the cavalry eventually arrived it was in the shape of Ben, a short bulbous bloke whose institutionalised brain left little room for anything you could call a personality. But he was efficient and wholly unflappable. Nudging Lauren aside, Ben got the system to come to heel within moments, but it was long enough for

Lauren to steal a glance at her phone. The message was from Josh.

Call me — urgent.

Her heart jumped as she read the message. *God, what's happened?* She wouldn't be off reception for another hour, but she couldn't wait that long to respond. *Damn!* Ben served several customers before handing the PC back to Lauren. She thought quickly.

"Ben, you couldn't hold the fort a bit longer could you? I need the toilet."

Ben stuck a finger in his ear and waggled it about, then ran a hand through a tangle of red curls that sat raggedly on the top of his head as if she'd asked him to solve some complex mathematical equation.

"How long will you be? I've all the Document Supply stuff to sort out before the postman arrives."

Anyone else would have been fine accepting Lauren's simple request, but Ben was somewhere near the top of the scale.

"I'll be as quick as I can," she said, noticing a stern-looking girl waiting at the desk.

"Well… okay… maybe for a couple of minutes."

"Thank you." Lauren turned on her heel before Ben had a chance to change his mind. She made for the staff room and called Josh.

"What's the matter; are you all right?"

Josh sounded edgy.

"I'm in a bit of a spot," he said. "Basically, I need somewhere to crash for a few days. I wondered if there was a chance of staying over at yours."

"What's happened?"

"I had another blast with Mum and Dad, and I finished up kipping in the car last night."

Lauren took a breath. "God. It must have been serious."

"It was over the flat. I told them I liked it and was seriously considering it. We all lost it a bit and I said a few things that maybe I shouldn't have done, but the top of it all is that I've walked out."

"And you slept in your *car*?"

"Yeah, I've had better nights I can tell you. I can't go back home, and I can't face another night on the back seat. It would just be for a couple of nights, what do you say?"

"I'll have to talk to Gran about it, but I'm sure everything will be all right."

"Cheers, Lauren, you're a star."

"I'll get back to you later. I'm supposed to be on reception at the minute so I can't do much about anything right now."

"Yeah, I get that."

"Okay. Speak to you soon, bye."

She called him at lunchtime with the good news.

"I knew you wouldn't let me down," Josh said. He was much brighter than when she'd spoken to him earlier in the morning. "And guess what? I've decided to take the flat we looked at yesterday."

"You *have*?" She was sitting on her favourite bench in the park, minus Pritvia who had reluctantly agreed to give Lauren some privacy while she spoke to Josh.

"It's a case of necessity. This bear ain't got anywhere to lay his head."

Lauren was struck dumb.

"Are you still there?"

"Yes. I'm sorry, I wasn't expecting you to have made your mind up so quickly."

"I know you don't like the place very much, but it's functional and it's within my budget."

"Have you spoken to your mum and dad yet?"

"No. But I'll tell them soon enough once the dust's settled a bit."

"I should do it now, Josh and get it all over with."

"I'll handle things in my own way, Lauren. I know what I'm doing."

"So when do you sign the papers?"

"It's done already. The boss let me off for a couple of hours to sort it all out."

"So you've got the keys?"

"I pick them up on Monday. There's a couple of sparkies coming to do some rewiring over the weekend so I'm leaving it until then."

"You're a fast mover, I'll give you that," Lauren said, hoping her tone didn't betray her doubts about how he was playing his cards. With her birthday party coming up on Sunday, she hoped that Josh would have everything ironed out with his parents; the last thing she wanted was for him to be distracted by the fractures of his parental estrangement or the possibility of him being pestered by them with phone calls. She was feeling edgy enough as it was, worrying how Josh was going to behave with Zak around.

"Trust me, Lauren, everything's going to be great. I'll see you at yours tonight."

10

O ne drawback of being the 'guest' of the house was that you didn't have much say of what TV you got to watch. It was nice having Lauren snuggled against you on the sofa, not so good with parents sitting like bookends in their armchairs on either side, but a reality TV programme that the household 'regulars' thought was hilarious was a bit of a stretch of Josh's patience. He would have preferred that the two of them had headed out somewhere, or at the very least gone up to Lauren's room where he could get his hands on her, but he had a feeling that a family ritual was taking place. Once he'd endured enough of the inane drivel on the box, he announced that he was ready to hit the sack. Lauren said she'd come up with him. When they reached the landing, Lauren took his hands and kissed him. She was smiling broadly and looked happy and relaxed, pleased to be in his company despite her wider reservations.

"I'm proud of you," she said to him. "None of this can be easy for you."

"You make it easier," Josh said, looking into her sparkling eyes. "I don't know where I'd be without you."

They kissed again.

"See you in the morning," Lauren said.

"I could get used to you saying that."

Josh was up early the next day. He raided the coffee and helped himself to cereals. There wasn't much to choose from. The breakfast choice was definitely female influenced, with healthy bars, muesli and low fat yoghurts. He eventually found some cornflakes pushed to the back of a cupboard. He heard footsteps padding down the stairs and was disappointed to see Lauren's grandad come through the door. Wrapped in a gown that did nothing to conceal his paunch, he wasn't easy on the eye at six in the morning.

"Morning, lad," he said as he made for the kettle. He grabbed two cups from a shelf and spooned generous amounts of coffee into each. He sat opposite Josh as the kettle rumbled slowly into life. He shifted on his seat, made a few noises and then said, "You'll not be rushing our Lauren into anything will you?"

Josh looked blankly at him. Geoff went on: "Lauren's a nice girl and she's growing up fast. We've never had any problems with her, and she's never brought trouble home. She's going to be a fine young lady. What I'm saying is, if you have any hopes for a future together, go slow. You know what I'm saying?"

Josh nodded.

"Good." Geoff slapped him on the shoulder and went over to wait for the kettle.

11

He should have known it would be a mistake to tell the lads at the garage about Geoff's 'advice' that he'd copped over breakfast. They'd been merciless in their piss-taking and the jokes had worn thin hours ago. Although he'd taken the punches on the chin, riding them out and retaliating with his own sarcastic remarks throughout the day, he was feeling rattled. It was probably as much to do with the row he'd had with his parents as it was with what the lads were saying, but whatever the underlying cause, he carried the feeling right until it was time to head off home. He'd no intention of spending the night at Lauren's in the mood of the devil and had already decided that the best way to lighten his spirits was to have a few bevvies down at the local.

The Robin Hood was well known for its decent ale, so it didn't surprise Josh to find the place reasonably busy, even at half past five. There were a few 'suits' in the place, probably legal people judging by their pompous behaviour, several old-timers and a group of lads flinging arrows at a dartboard in the corner. Josh went to the bar and was served by a middle-aged cleavage on legs. He asked for a lager much to the consternation of a wiry bloke propping up the far end of the bar.

"You're drinking piss when there's nectar on flow," he said above the din. Josh noticed the guy was drinking some sort of real ale judging by the colour of what was in his pint glass.

"What the fuck's it got to do with you?"

"Don't start anything, Pete," the cleavage said. "It's all nectar here." She handed Josh his pint. He necked it back quickly. Pete came alongside him, reeking of stale cigs and ale. He was an ugly git for sure with a nose that could have hooked fish, and a chin as sharp as flint. Josh reckoned the guy was around fifty, but he was probably younger.

"I haven't seen you in here before," Pete said, draining his pint and signalling to the cleavage he wanted a refill.

Josh shrugged without comment.

"I said I haven't seen you—"

"I heard you the first time," Josh said irritably.

"Where I come from when people speak it's polite to answer."

Josh turned to face the man square on.

"I've had a shitty enough day without people sticking their oar into my business. I just want a quiet drink and then I'll be off your patch."

Before Pete could respond, the cleavage took his glass and started to fill it.

"Take no notice, love," she said to Josh as she worked the pump. "When he's bored he likes to wind folk up. Pity he hasn't anything better to do."

"Well, that's up to you, Janice," Pete said. "I'm sure you could keep me suitably entertained."

Janice pulled a face and handed Pete his pint. "Four pounds," she said, thrusting an open hand in front of him.

Pete dug into his pocket and gave her a tenner.

"I could fuck her till she begged me to stop," he said to Josh as Janice went to the till.

"Each to their own."

"You got a lady?"

"Yeah."

"Good between the sheets is she?"

"What the fuck's it got to do with you?"

Janice placed Pete's change on the bar. He scooped it up without counting and stuffed it into his trouser pocket.

"You're a touchy sod aren't you?" Pete said, taking a gulp of his fresh pint.

Josh knew he should just walk away. The guy was obviously pissed and looking to spark a reaction. It was the easiest and safest option to take. Perhaps if he hadn't been feeling so shitty he might have done. But he didn't. Instead, he belted the guy square across the jaw. Pete was caught off guard and staggered into the wall but stayed upright despite his slender build. His retaliation for a man who'd obviously downed a few impressed the bystanders who had little intention of stopping the entertainment and he launched a rangy fist that caught Josh full in his left eye. Josh only just stayed on his feet, reeling under the blow, however his counterpunch was pretty good, landing on Pete's invitingly jutting chin, but still the guy didn't go down, though he was certainly unsteady now. Pete rubbed his bleeding mouth and spat out what looked like a tooth. Janice was yelling something from the back of the bar, which stirred a couple of the 'suits' to intervene and halt the fight in its tracks before it could escalate any further.

"Get them both out of here," Janice said. "You're barred, both of you."

Josh pushed the 'suit' away from him.

"Get your fucking hands off me; I know where the door is."

The 'suit', clearly not wanting to cop a belt himself, allowed Josh to pass without argument. Once outside, Josh could feel his eye begin to swell. Catching his reflection in a nearby shop window, he saw that it was already beginning to close. *Fuck! I'm going to look like shit when I get to Lauren's.* When he got back to his car he was better able to assess the damage. Yes, his eye had seen better days for sure, but apart from that there were no cuts or torn clothing. He'd have to pass it off as some sort of accident at work.

He got back to Lauren's half an hour later. She'd only just got in herself, and immediately commented on his bruised eye.

"It looks nasty," she said, smoothing a gentle hand around the swelling. "Do you want some painkillers?"

Josh shook his head. "I'm all right. It looks worse than it feels."

"How did it happen?"

Josh liked the concern etched on her face. He'd half a mind to play up to it.

"The end bit of a torque wrench came loose," he lied. "Flew up and smacked me in the eye."

"Ouch! It must have hurt."

Iris, who was milling around in the kitchen, announced that dinner would be ready in half an hour and was sure Josh would like to get himself 'cleaned up'. Josh took the hint and dashed upstairs. Lauren went through into the kitchen. Dinner smelled good.

"I thought we'd have a treat," Iris said, proudly. "It's Chicken Marsala. I found the recipe on the internet."

"You've finally got the hang of the tablet then have you?"

Iris shrugged. "I'm getting there."

"It smells great."

"Are you and Josh going out tonight?"

"I expect so, though we won't be staying out late; he's working in the morning."

"Your grandad said he wouldn't be too late, so we'll probably be eating together." They heard a car turn into the driveway. "In fact, that's probably him now. And while I think on," Iris said, "it would be a help if you went into town for me tomorrow morning. Your grandad and me are going over to your Aunty Vanessa's, so I've a list of things I need you to get from the butchers. It's all things for your birthday on Sunday."

Lauren didn't mind, especially as it was for her benefit, besides, it got her out of a trip to her Aunty Vanessa's, a somewhat overpowering personality that was only dwarfed by her pudgy frame. Aunty Vanessa was all right in small doses, the smaller the better.

Geoff was in a good mood when he came in; affectionately kissed both wife and granddaughter on the cheek, then good-naturedly bemoaned the fact that he'd struggled to get his car into the drive because Josh had parked there.

"It's worse than Morrison's on a Saturday afternoon," he said.

When Josh came down just before dinner was due to be served, Geoff quickly appraised his shiner.

"Somebody belted you?' he said, unaware of just how close to the truth he was.

Josh fobbed him off with the same answer he'd given to both Lauren and Iris.

"It's a wonder it didn't cut you," Geoff said.

"I guess I was lucky," Josh replied, stoically.

"It's rare that metal doesn't produce blood, especially around the eye."

Josh sensed that Geoff had more than a good idea that the bruise had been caused by someone's fist but was saved further defensive work by Iris calling everyone through for dinner. He was glad of Lauren's trivial conversation as they ate, how she went on and on about what had happened at work (it sounded like her day lacked anything resembling graft) and how quickly she could jump from one subject to the next. If you weren't concentrating, you'd quickly get lost. It was only a matter of time before the subject of her birthday party reared its head, which reminded him that he'd left the presents he'd bought her at his mum and dad's. He'd got her some wireless earbuds for her phone, a bottle of Gucci perfume and a Michael Kors purse. All in all it had all come in at just under two hundred quid, and it was all shoved under his bed and yet to be wrapped. Still, he had to face his parents some time. (He had in fact messaged his mum to tell her he was staying over at Lauren's, but she hadn't replied, which didn't bode well.) But that was tomorrow's concern. There was the evening to enjoy first, and Lauren was a more than adequate distraction.

12

The middle-aged man had not intended to go into town on Saturday morning, but when he recognised Lauren's blue Corsa heading down the hill to Pontefract, he felt the overwhelming compulsion to follow, reasoning it was an opportunity too good to miss. His wife, Kate, wasn't with him and the sacks of compost he was supposedly picking up from the garden centre could wait a bit longer. He was careful to maintain a covert distance from Lauren, but hawkishly watched her every turn. She was a confident driver, he noticed, positive and assured, perhaps a little too quick at times. The roads were busy, and he thought he might lose her when they came to the major roundabout at the bottom of the hill, but he noticed her heading straight on into the town centre, even though he had to wait for several cars passing from the right. Once clear, he kicked down on the accelerator and picked up speed until she came into view again. It looked as if she was making for a large municipal car park. When he saw an orange indicator winking a left turn from the main road, he knew his hunch was correct. He slowed down and took the same left himself.

The car park was half full. Even though it was the main shopping day for most people, Pontefract hadn't really sprung back into life after lockdown and was only ever half-awake these days. He noted where she parked her car and chose a space just outside the range of her peripheral vision. He watched as she got out of her car and crossed to the parking meter. He liked her flowing yellow dress, the bag slung over her shoulder and how she wore her hair in a long tail. She was reading a notice on the meter and pushed a button for a ticket. When she returned to her car, he decided it was time to make a move. He picked up a ticket of his own, not daring to take his eyes off the girl, stuck it onto his windscreen and then followed her into town. He kept at a safe distance, watched her go into the indoor market that adjoined the car park and duly pursued. He saw that she was perusing what he assumed was a shopping list before making her way over to a butcher's stall. The man dug out his mobile, carefully engaged the camera, selected video and started to record. He followed her as she left the market and headed out across the main shopping precinct to Mason's bakery shop. He'd no chance of recording her in there, so he pretended to look in the windows of nearby shops until she re-emerged, carrying a large bag of pastries. He continued to follow and track her, saw that she paused outside Shakespeare's Café before deciding to go in. It was quite a rustic olde time place, very popular with the locals and today was no exception, but there were still vacant tables. He peered through the window to see where she was sitting. Every fibre of his being ached to follow her inside.

He thought hard for a few moments, bore the incredible pain of yearning that seared through him as he pondered what to do. There was a table just to her left. His heart started to race. He couldn't miss this opportunity. He would be so close to her!

Bugger it; I'm going in, he declared silently to himself.

The strong aroma of ground coffee hit him as he entered. The rattle of cups, plates and cutlery made the place feel extra homely and vibrant. He quickly chose his seat and went through the motions of looking at the menu. He stole a glance in Lauren's direction. She was browsing over the menu. When a young waitress eventually came across, he heard her order an Americano and a chocolate muffin. When the waitress took his order, he opted for a flat white, and skipped the food. Lauren was now looking at her phone. She didn't seem to have noticed him, but being noticed wasn't his objective. It was enough to be in her presence. He pretended to look at his phone. He could see out of his peripheral vision that she was texting someone. He was amazed how the younger generation could tap out messages at light speed. She caught his eye. There was little doubt in his mind that she showed some sign of recognition. His heart skipped a few beats. Her expression was not prepossessing, and she seemed to be biting down on her lip as if caught in thought. He looked away and concentrated on his phone and flat white. He realised his hand was trembling. Within five minutes, Lauren left the café. He did not follow her. Instead, he scrolled to his gallery images and

began to inspect what he'd managed to record and liked
what he saw.

13

Lauren hadn't taken kindly to seeing the man in the café. She wanted to put his presence down to coincidence, but in her heart she knew that idea was cock and bull. His table selection told her that for one thing. She'd no idea that he'd been following her around town of course, much less recording images of her. (Had she have had any inkling of this she'd have been terrified.) As it was, her predominant feelings were ones of unease. Seeing him in the café had come as a bit of a shock and it had ruined her coffee. To add to her discomfort, she still had a few more items of shopping to get. She also wanted to drop off a fresh sandwich for Josh at the garage. He didn't work every Saturday, but she'd promised him a small treat, as he'd seemed preoccupied at the pub last night. She supposed it was to do with his impending move and estrangement from his parents and wanted to raise his spirits a bit.

She rushed through the remainder of the shopping, checking over her shoulder every now and again, but she saw no sign of the man. Why did she always catch his eye whenever he was around? It didn't matter whether it was on the train, in the Co-op, or in a café. Their eyes always met as if they were somehow laser guided. Could it be that he was simply registering a familiar face? It was possible, but that didn't answer why she'd seen him apparently pointing his phone towards her on occasion. She toyed with the idea of telling her grandad about what she was thinking but dismissed the idea almost straightaway. The man had never behaved in a threatening manner or made any approach for one thing. It would be difficult to justify airing her concerns without actually having some direct proof that the man was stalking her, if stalking was even the right word. She shuddered at the thought and grabbed at the idea that she was misreading things. Besides, if she made a complaint without getting her facts right, she could end up in trouble herself. She'd got a bit of form after all and that had killed her friendship with Michelle Carter. It wasn't worth the risk.

Within the hour, she was driving to Josh's garage, which was at the lower end of town, not too far from Pontefract train station. She called in at a local sandwich shop and ordered him a ham salad on a large brown bread bun and bought herself a tuna and mayonnaise sandwich that she could hardly wait for. To top off the order, she also bought a couple of cans of iced coffee. She messaged Josh to let him know she was on her way, hoping that he'd be able to sneak off for half an hour so they could spend a bit of time together.

It was Josh's boss who saw Lauren pull into the parking area. Vaguely aware that Josh was expecting a visitor, he yelled into the back, "Your lass is here, Josh."

Josh ambled into the reception area wiping his hands on a dirty rag. He waved to Lauren as she got out of the car. He signalled 'two minutes' and she nodded and waited.

"Pretty girl," his boss said.

"Yeah," Josh said. "She scrubs up."

"What's she see in you?"

Josh winked. "That'd be telling." He went to the toilet to wash his hands as clean as he could get them, however, no matter how hard he scoured and rubbed, he could never get rid of the smell of Swarfega. When he returned, he was in his tee shirt and shorts.

"You've got forty minutes," his boss said.

Josh nodded. "Cheers."

They sat on a grassy bank and filled their rumbling stomachs. Whereas Josh had been the one who was preoccupied last night, now it was Lauren's turn.

"You all right?" he asked, cracking open his can of coffee.

"Yes," Lauren nodded, flashing him a bright smile that she hoped didn't look forced.

"You don't seem yourself."

"Sorry," she said, wondering if it would be a good idea to tell Josh about the middle-aged man rather than her grandparents. "I've just got a few things on my mind, that's all."

"What sort of things?"

Lauren hesitated before opting out, remembering the risk. "Nothing, really."

"It must be something to keep you quiet. Usually I have to fight to get a word in edgeways."

"Josh, it really is nothing," she said, already thinking she'd said enough. "Don't push it, please."

"Fair enough," Josh shrugged. They sat quietly for a minute or two. Josh got to his feet. "C'mon," he said. "Let's go for a walk. It might brighten you up a bit." He offered his hand and pulled her up. "I should be able to knock off at half three," he said. "It'll make things less rushed for tonight."

Lauren paused for a moment and kicked some grit from her sandal.

"I'd like to go somewhere quiet," she said. "Maybe out to a country pub."

"Sounds good," Josh said. "I'll treat you to a pre-birthday drink. At least I'll have you all to myself tonight."

She kissed him and then hugged him tightly.

"Steady on," he said. "I've got to breathe!"

She buried her head into his chest and revelled in the smell of chemicals and motor oil. She felt protected, safe.

When Josh finished his shift, he headed straight for his parents' house. (He certainly wasn't going to call it home any more.) Acutely aware that he'd probably be as popular as pig shit once he got there, he was nevertheless prepared to play the 'prodigal son', albeit briefly, and if he could get out of the place without his ears being severely bent, he'd count it a successful mission. He half hoped that they wouldn't be home, but as Sod's Law would have it, they were in. He pulled into the driveway and parked directly behind his dad's Astra. He could already feel the adrenaline pumping through his veins as his last parting shot to his dad replayed in his brain, *"Go fuck yourself!"* He regretted the choice of words now, if not his actions, but what was done was done. They'd probably both have something to say about his shiner, too. They wouldn't be fobbed off with the torque wrench bull that he'd given Lauren that was for sure.

He took a couple of breaths before he entered the cauldron, was tempted to dash straight upstairs to his room, grab Lauren's presents and then hoof it, but he could hear them both in the living room, so he decided to front it out. It wasn't as if he hadn't done it before. His dad was cutting his toenails over a newspaper spread out on the carpet and his mum was reading a magazine while the TV played to no one.

"I've come for Lauren's presents," Josh said. "Just in case you wondered why I came back."

His dad stopped clipping his nails. "I hardly thought you'd come to apologise," he said looking red in the face. Josh couldn't tell whether it was because he'd caught the sun or whether the blood had rushed to his face with bending to reach his toes.

"That works both ways," Josh said, determined not to take full blame for their rift.

"It's not us that needs to wash our mouths out either," Josh's dad said, severely. "Talking of mouths, it looks like yours got you a good hiding too, something you probably had coming."

"Whatever," Josh said, seeing little point in proclaiming the fact that he'd been provoked into the fight that had left its obvious mark.

Josh's dad went back to cutting his nails. His mum stared with narrow eyes at her magazine.

Josh shifted on his feet, waiting for someone to speak but it soon became apparent that no one had anything further to say, so he said: "I took the flat, just so you know. I'll be back on Monday for all my stuff."

He went to his room and gathered Lauren's presents. He hadn't even wrapped them yet and it wasn't a job he was going to do here, so he'd have to nip into town, get the necessaries and sort it all out in the privacy of his car. Not ideal, but it was part of the price for shooting your mouth off. As he trudged back downstairs, he could clearly see the door to freedom. Although elated that he'd finally secured a place of his own, he was disappointed that his parents couldn't be pleased for him. *"You're throwing your money away, as well as your brain,"* his dad had said, kicking off the whole argument in the first place.

"It's somewhere to call my own, so I don't have you two pushing and controlling me twenty-four seven."

"You're thinking with your dick, this is about that lass you're knocking off. I suppose she's put you up to this."

"Leave Lauren out of it."

"You'll never have money chucking brass away on rent."

"And if I save for a deposit, I might get away from here in about 2040, if I'm lucky!"

And now he was out, breathing in the summer air.

"There's ways to save if you use your bloody grey stuff."

"Go fuck yourself!"

And that had been it. If he hadn't quite sunk his boat, it was certainly taking in water.

14

Lauren drove them both out to Heath Common, an idyllic beauty spot half an hour from home on the outskirts of Wakefield. The main attraction apart from the expansive meadows and surrounding flora was the rustic pub that served real ales and fantastic food. Lauren hadn't been here since her grandparents had brought her to celebrate passing her driving test eighteen months ago. The popular beer garden that took in the panoramic views was busy, not rowdy. Lauren was happy to sit outside. Young families were enjoying themselves; dogs scampered and barked here and there, chasing sticks and balls or anything else they could tear after. Josh ordered the drinks while Lauren relaxed at a vacant table, gazing at the amber sky as the sun slowly dipped over the distant hills. For one horrible moment she thought she saw the middle-aged man and a woman she supposed was his wife at a nearby table, but she was thankfully mistaken. One of the reasons she'd wanted to go a bit further afield tonight was to avoid any chance encounter with the man, though when she thought about it, she'd never yet seen him in a pub. By the time Josh came back with their drinks, she'd recovered her composure. He sat beside her, and she immediately took his hand and kissed him on the cheek.

"What is it with you today?" he asked, enjoying the affection that Lauren was openly showing him.

"I can kiss you can't I?"

"Yeah, of course, I'm not complaining."

"Good," she said. "Because there's plenty more of where they came from."

Josh took a swig of his beer.

"It's been lovely having you to stay," Lauren said. "I think Grandad's enjoyed it too. It's been a long time since he wasn't outnumbered."

"He will be from Monday," Josh said.

"Yes, your first day of independence."

"I'm only doing what I have to do. You're still coming round after work aren't you?"

"Of course I am."

"You can stay over whenever you want."

Lauren bit on her lip. "I know that Josh. And I will, I promise."

Josh looked down into his drink. "I love you, Lauren," he said, his tone suddenly earnest. "I'd do anything for you, I really would."

Lauren felt her eyes prickle. "They're the nicest words I've heard in a long time. Thank you." She kissed him on the cheek. His expression was still serious. Now it was her turn to ask if something was wrong.

"I was just thinking about Mum and Dad that's all," Josh replied. "Why can't they be pleased for me, Lauren?"

It was a good question and one she couldn't answer.

"I'm sure they'll come round in the end," she said, gently stroking his hand. How difficult it must be to be alienated from your parents, she thought. How deep the rift was, only time would tell.

"He used to belt me you know, when I was younger," Josh said out of the blue.

"Oh my God, that's awful," Lauren said, clearly stunned at the revelation.

"Tell me about it."

"What did you do to deserve being hit?" Lauren asked, before adding, "Not that anyone ever deserves to be hit of course."

"Little things, mainly," Josh said. "Kicking a ball into a flowerbed, being late home, muddy trousers, that kind of thing. He only really stopped as I got older, and he realised that if I hit back he'd probably come off worse. Dad once told me that I was a mistake, an unhappy accident. He was leathering me at the time. Sometimes I think I should have just run away."

"I can't believe your dad said that. Do you think he really meant it?"

Josh shrugged. "He said it, that's enough. I've never forgotten it."

"No wonder you want to get out. They've always been kind to me."

"Painted faces, Lauren, painted faces."

15

The house was in darkness when Lauren turned into the driveway.

"In bed already?" Josh said, slightly the worse for wear.

"It's past midnight," Lauren said. "And we've got a busy day, remember?"

"Oh, yeah, I'd forgotten. It's Sunday today. Happy birthday!"

Lauren killed the engine and planted a kiss on Josh's cheek. "Thank you. C'mon. And don't make too much noise."

Once they got inside, Josh pulled Lauren into the living room. They embraced and kissed. The watery light of a street lamp seeped through a slit in the curtains, so that each could see the other's eyes sparkling like diamonds. Josh smoothed his hand around the contours of Lauren's face. She took him by the hand and led him upstairs.

"We'll have to be very quiet," she whispered.

16

Josh had no idea what time it was when he slunk from Lauren's room. He crept stealthily along the landing to his room, the floorboards creaking conspiratorially in places even though he was in his bare feet. He fumbled for the handle and pushed open the door. Before he managed to step inside, a sudden blinding light forced him to shield his eyes. He spun quickly on his heels and looked straight into the glowering eyes of Lauren's grandad.

17

I t was not the birthday anyone had envisaged. In fact, it would be one that would go down in the memory for all the wrong reasons. Virtually from the off things were not good. Lauren had naturally been looking forward to this day for weeks, the final shedding of her teenage years for the kudos of entering her twenties. Not that her teenage years had been bad (except when she had her first bleed at thirteen — catapulting her out of childhood into the choppy waters of adolescence) but your twenties generally signalled the inevitability of big change if you were open to it.

She'd been given her presents before breakfast. (A Topshop voucher worth £100, a new hair dryer, two tee shirts, some Viktor and Rolf perfume — and of course the gifts that Josh had bought for her.) She was genuinely thrilled by everyone's generosity, but the whole affair had been tense with forced politeness and it was obvious why. Geoff might not have caught Josh with his pants down, but it was pretty damned obvious that they'd been somewhere round his ankles only minutes before he'd seen him sneaking back to his room. It wasn't as if Geoff or Iris were so naïve to think that Lauren was still a virgin, or that they didn't recognise the flaming passion of youth, but the thought of those passions being played out under their own roof did not sit easily, particularly when they were in the room next door. Perhaps the Jurassic attitude that Pritvia had pointed out to Lauren not so long ago was born of the fact that neither Geoff nor Iris overly relished the fact that Lauren was rapidly becoming 'a woman'.

Breakfast itself was certainly strained, where words were at a premium. Both Lauren and Josh were sheepish and embarrassed. Lauren would have preferred the mother of all lectures rather than bear the disappointed looks on the faces of her grandparents. If it wasn't her special day, she might well have borne some censure already, but as it was, the disapproval that reluctantly hid behind the affected faces of her grandparents remained an ominous threat, and one that had pissed on the fire of the 'happy birthday' wishes they'd bestowed on her as they'd presented her with her gifts. For Josh, Monday could hardly come quickly enough. When Geoff said that he needed a hand putting up the gazebo for the party it was obvious whom he was expecting to help.

Lauren was left in the kitchen with her gran.

"There's some salad to prepare," Iris said sharply. (The party might have been for Lauren's benefit, but it didn't get her out of helping with the preparations.)

"And then there's the vol-au-vents to make up."

Lauren went over to the fridge and pulled out various bags of salad. She put them on the work surface and started to sort out what needed washing and chopping. Her gran's continual air of disapproval was worse than a raging storm. In the end Lauren said, "Will you just say what it is you want to say. I've had enough of the dagger-eyes, thank you."

Iris was not impressed with Lauren's show of spirit.

"And I will thank you not to talk to me in that tone, young lady. I really thought you two could have exercised some self-control, I'm surprised at you, Lauren."

"It's hardly a crime, Gran."

"That's not the point! It's a matter of respecting the rules of this house. Really, Lauren, I never thought I'd have to have this conversation with you."

"Oh, come on, Gran, it's not as if we haven't slept together before!" Her voice was still raised.

"I'm talking about what you get up to in this house and keep your voice down!"

Lauren took her frustration out on the lettuce, ripping the leaves from the stem.

Her gran went on: "I don't know what he said to persuade you into doing what you did, but all I can say is that it's a good job he's out of here tomorrow."

Lauren slammed the knife she was holding down onto the workspace.

"It was me, Gran! *I* said he could come to my room."

Iris was aghast, not so much at Lauren's words, but by her hostility. Without thinking, she slapped the girl across the face. There was a terrible silence as they both tried to comprehend what had just happened. Already Iris was

mortified by her action.

"Oh, Lauren," she sobbed. "I'm so sorry."

But it was too late. Lauren fled tearfully from the kitchen.

18

"We couldn't help ourselves," Josh said, assisting Geoff as he spread the canvas awning on the lawn. "I know it was a bit of a liberty, but... well we're young and red-blooded."

Geoff pulled out the gazebo's support poles from the kit bag.

"Did anything I said to you the other morning sink in?"

Josh didn't have time to answer as Iris came flying out of the house.

"I've done something terrible!" she wailed.

"What?" Geoff said.

Iris was crying openly.

"Go to her, please. Tell her I'm sorry."

"What are you talking about?"

She blurted out what she had done. "I feel terrible! I didn't mean it."

Geoff cursed. "This place has turned into a bloody madhouse." He started to make his way indoors.

"I'll go," Josh said. "I'm not being funny, but I don't think she'll want to talk to you."

"And you'd know, would you?"

"Well it isn't me she's angry with."

Geoff wrestled with Josh's words, wanting to resist them, but he knew Josh was right.

"Okay," he spat. "Go to her."

Josh was up to Lauren's room in a flash. He rapped on the door.

"Go away!" Lauren yelled.

"It's me, Josh."

Lauren immediately opened the door and flung her arms around him with such force that he staggered to take her weight. She was weeping bitterly, trying to speak, but her sobs made her words incomprehensible.

"Lauren, I can't tell what you're saying. C'mon, let's sit on the bed. Have you got some tissues?"

Lauren sniffled and nodded. Josh had never seen her cry before, not properly. He'd wondered how he might react when he did. The reality choked him. To actually look directly into eyes that were streaming tears of heartbreak forced him to dig deep to hold his own emotions in check. He couldn't think of what to say, so he held her until she finally started to compose herself.

"This is all my fault," Josh said. "If I hadn't been here, none of this would have happened."

"Don't you say that," Lauren sobbed and blew her nose. He could feel her body trembling against his.

"You know you can't stay up here all day, you're supposed to be the star of the show," he said

"I can't just pretend nothing's happened," Lauren complained.

"If it's any consolation, your gran's pretty cut up about it." This revelation set Lauren off crying again. "It might be better if I find somewhere else to lay my head tonight," Josh went on. "All things considered."

"No!" Lauren was aghast at the idea. "Anyway, you've nowhere to go."

"I could maybe doss down with one of the lads from work. Failing that, kip in the car."

"You're staying here, Josh."

"It might not be up to me. Your grandad's already given me one yellow card, the next's a red."

"What do you mean?" Lauren sniffed and blew her nose again, not picking up on the football metaphor.

Josh told her about the friendly advice Geoff had given him on Friday.

"He did what?"

"Don't make a deal of it, Lauren. You'll make things worse."

She buried her head in her hands. This was unbelievable.

"God, what a birthday!"

"I think you should dry your eyes and make it up with your gran," Josh said. "You've got everyone coming this afternoon, you're going to have to show your face."

Lauren nodded, trying to muster some spirit. "I know."

Josh planted a kiss on her forehead. "That's my girl," he said.

The second that Lauren caught sight of her gran the floodgates opened again. The pair embraced with heartfelt apologies and tears that poured like the rain. Josh let them have their privacy and went to find Geoff. He was still in the garden sorting out the gazebo.

"They'll both be fine," Josh said, picking up one of the support poles and sticking it in the ground.

Geoff eyed him diffidently. "That's all right then." They worked together for a few minutes in silence.

"I love her you know," Josh said as the last of the posts was fixed down.

Geoff nodded. He was still annoyed with the lad but didn't dislike him.

"The awning can be a bit fiddly," he said. "My fault for getting a cheap model."

Josh sniggered. "With a BMW on the drive something had to give, eh?"

Geoff grudgingly smiled.

They worked together, slightly easier now. Geoff could see how practical Josh was, how good he was at working things out, the tetchy loops and threads that were often a struggle for him was plain sailing for Josh. Within twenty minutes the gazebo was fully erected and tethered.

"A job well done!" Geoff said, appraising their handiwork.

"You should see me with engines," Josh replied.

Geoff allowed himself a chuckle. He slapped Josh on the shoulder. "It's been a bit of a morning," he said. He led Josh away from the house and into the garage. He pulled out a couple of cans of beer from the fridge in the corner, and tossed one over to Josh. They cracked them open.

"One day she's going to fly the nest," Geoff said. "Sooner rather than later, perhaps. Doesn't seem two minutes since she was at school. When the time comes, it's not going to be easy to let her go."

Josh took a gulp of his beer. "We're not going to rush anything if that's what you're worried about."

"Well, if your nocturnal jaunt last night was an example of going slow, heaven help us when you get a sprint on."

They both laughed.

"C'mon, let's see what the girls are up to," Geoff said.

19

The afternoon was hot. The entourage of friends (average age nineteen, mainly attractive young ladies in summer dresses) were being well entertained with free-flowing wine, sandwiches and pastries. Lauren seemed to have recovered from the morning and playing the role of assistant hostess to her own party helped her to focus on the pleasanter things. Pritvia, as ebullient as ever, swirling like a dervish in a brilliant red dress, couldn't keep her eyes off Josh who was helping with the drinks.

He's not a bad looking lad, she thought. *Lauren has done well. Maybe I should try this internet dating lark.* He was better looking in the flesh, selfies didn't do anyone justice. His shiner seemed to give him something extra too; it certainly wasn't doing his charm and sex appeal any damage. She clocked several girls giving him the once over and felt a sting of jealousy rise in her. He made the odd humorous remark in response to some flirtatious comment, and giddy laughter usually followed. Pritvia collared him and introduced herself boldly as Lauren's best friend, that she'd heard lots about him and that finally meeting him in person was not a disappointment. Josh, still enjoying lots of female attention, soon soured when Zak arrived laden with flowers for both Lauren and her gran and was subsequently showered with hugs and kisses. Zak, utterly oblivious to Josh's untrusting eyes, more or less picked up from where he'd left off the last time he'd seen her. Josh understood that he would have to share Lauren this afternoon, but as time passed, he realised that Zak was like a limpet, always in her presence, and she was doing little to discourage him. It was clear to Josh that Zak was a good friend of the family too; both of Lauren's grandparents seemed to think the world of him, as well as some of the guests who already knew him. Pritvia kept close to Josh for a good half hour, her budding intuition sensing that the lad was becoming increasingly restless, and it hadn't taken long for her to work out why.

"You should let her enjoy herself," she said as Josh watched the pair go into the kitchen, laughing and giggling like kids together. "It isn't every day you celebrate your birthday."

Why don't you piss off out of my hair, he thought. *You're like bloody glue.*

"Bet you can't wait to get her to your new place," Pritvia teased, flashing a toothy grin.

"News travels fast," Josh said, not sounding overly friendly. "I suppose she's told you everything about me."

"That's what girls generally do."

"What's she being saying about me then?"

Pritvia tapped her nose. "That would be telling."

Josh smiled without humour. "Girls and their secrets, eh?"

Pritvia shrugged. "I bet you've got quite a few secrets stashed away in that head of yours."

"Now who's being nosey?"

She could tell that Josh wanted to get away from her and was preoccupied with what was going on in the kitchen.

"You don't like the little guy much do you?"

"Not especially."

"Take a chill pill, you've got nothing to worry about."

"Who said I was worried?"

"You don't like her being with him."

"Who are you, Miss fucking Marple?"

Pritvia raised her eyebrows above the rim of her large glasses.

"Hmm, a touchy sort aren't you?"

"Why don't you get yourself another drink and bother somebody else?"

If his words hurt her, she didn't show it. "You know, you should put some shades over those green eyes of yours, maybe it'll hide the monster as well as your bruise."

"Leave it, eh?"

"You're nothing like I thought you'd be."

"Well, you know what thought did."

"How much have you been drinking?"

"You're my mother now are you?"

Pritvia shook her head.

"If I was your mother, I'd have slapped you by now."

"Read my lips, fuck off."

Pritvia held his gaze for a few moments before turning away and heading over to the gazebo where Geoff was stoically acting as barman, still topping up endless glasses of wine and beer.

"And fucking stay over there you nosey cow," Josh said under his breath. He went straight for the kitchen, under Pritvia's glaring gaze.

"What the hell's going on here?" Josh blurted out as he caught Lauren and Zak in an affectionate embrace.

The pair immediately broke apart. Lauren's large eyes locked onto Josh in surprise.

"A private little party is it?" he added, coming right across.

"We were just hugging," Lauren said. "Zak's got to go soon."

Josh rounded on the little guy. "You're a bit too familiar for my liking. Are you after her or something?"

"Josh, stop it," Lauren said.

"Or maybe your special little friendship is a closed shop, is that it?" He grabbed Zak by the collar and pushed him aside. Zak staggered and clattered into the kitchen table. A couple of pieces of cutlery fell to the floor with a loud clash.

"We weren't doing anything," Zak complained defensively.

"It's not what it looked like."

Josh turned to Lauren. "What is it when you two get together? Folk need a battering ram to break you apart."

Lauren was not in the most robust of minds and he could see her eyes filling with tears.

"Josh don't do this," she said, fighting the knot in her throat.

Although oiled on beer, Josh wasn't so far gone that he couldn't see Lauren was becoming upset.

"I've told you before, Lauren, I'm not being shit to his piss, you just remember that." He turned and stormed out of the kitchen.

"I'm sorry," Lauren said when he'd gone. "He's been drinking." She was beginning to succumb to her tears. Zak eased her into a chair.

"I think you should be careful," he said. "He seems a bit dangerous to me."

Lauren shook her head. "No, he's usually very sweet," she sniffed. "It's just the drink."

"Drink only brings out what's already there, Lauren."

Josh slunk moodily into the garden and immediately caught Pritvia's wrath.

"If you wanted to screw up somebody's birthday party, you've done a damned good job. What the hell's wrong with you?"

"Do me a favour, fuck off." Josh said.

Pritvia was indignant.

"Lauren's my best friend and I'm looking out for her, you hear? She deserves better than you."

"What do you know about anything?"

"I know enough to see that you're going to be trouble for her."

"And you're going to get into trouble sticking your tits in where they're not wanted."

"You need to go back into that kitchen and apologise for what you just did."

"Christ almighty!"

"What the hell were you thinking?"

Josh got to his feet. Pritvia took a step away from him, unsure whether he might lash out at her, too. He could see that she was a bit wary of him now, he liked that, meant that she ultimately knew her place.

"I love her," he said, but there was no romance in his voice.

Pritvia shot him a smouldering look.

"Yours is the kind of love she can do without."

20

The final guests left at around seven. The tidying was a laborious job that seemed to take an age. Lauren and her gran sorted through the leftovers and washing up, while Geoff saw to all of the rubbish and empty bottles as Josh took down the gazebo. Afterwards Josh sat outside watching the sun sink in the distance, draining the last of his can. (He must have sunk ten today, but he wasn't counting.)

Thank God I'm not at work in the morning, he thought to himself. He became aware of someone standing behind him. He looked over his shoulder and saw that it was Lauren.

"What you did to Zak was unforgiveable," she said, curtly. "You're lucky Gran and Grandad didn't hear about it."

Josh said nothing.

"He's my friend, Josh."

"And what am I when he's around? Some sort of puppy dog you can just tell to run along and play?"

"I'm not arguing with you about it. I'm just telling you that's all."

"Well now you've told me."

She turned and left him.

Josh crunched his can and flung it to the far side of the garden.

21

J osh was up early the next morning. He expected to have a thick head, but he was surprised to find that he was bright and alert. He supposed it was the adrenaline. Today was the big day. Real independence at last. He sauntered into the kitchen and filled the kettle. He checked the time. It was six o'clock. He plonked himself by the table and ruminated on yesterday's events. It had certainly been a strange day and a particularly tough one for Lauren. As far as birthdays went it was a bit of a stinker. He knew he'd be in for some frosty treatment when Lauren emerged and thought long and hard how he might manage to instigate a quick thaw.

She came down at half past six as Josh was eating some cereal. She breezed almost ethereally past him still in her nightie.

"Morning," Josh said, knowing his bright tone wouldn't be appreciated.

"Morning," Lauren said, the predicted cold front clearly evident in her tone. She clicked the kettle on and rummaged in the cupboard for something to eat. She grabbed a breakfast bar.

"About yesterday…" Josh started.

"I've got to get ready for work."

"Can you at least let me explain?"

"Josh, it's half past six. My train goes in an hour."

"Tonight then. At my place." It actually felt good to say that despite the circumstances. *My place.* "You said you would."

The kettle boiled; Lauren quickly poured herself a coffee. "I'm going to get changed." She took her coffee out with her.

"I'll call you," Josh said.

Lauren didn't waste much time in going over yesterday's events with Pritvia during morning break.

"You need to watch out," Pritvia said. "There's something about him that's not right."

They were in the staff room drinking coffee; the other staff members lounging around were too busy with their own conversations to eavesdrop.

"I know he can be funny when he's had a few down him," Lauren said, desperate to rationalise Josh's behaviour, "but he's been under a lot of pressure at home."

"He screwed up your party, Lauren."

"The day had been screwed up long before the party, believe me."

"What do you mean?"

"I don't want to talk about it, but it wasn't anything that Josh did."

"I'm worried for you, Lauren."

"I'll be all right."

"You don't look it."

"Thanks."

"I want you to know that I'm always here for you. Any time."

"I know."

"So are you still going round to his new place tonight?"

Lauren sighed. "I'm going to ring him at lunchtime, he's got a lot of explaining to do."

"Make him grovel," Pritvia said, bitterly.

When Lauren called Josh, she found his manner contrite and somewhat sheepish.

"It won't happen again, I promise. I'll apologise to him if it makes you happy."

Lauren pressed her phone against her ear as a passing truck thundered by.

"And what about the next time you have a drink?" She cut across the road and headed into the park.

"I'll give it up if that's what you want."

"I want you to accept that I've got friends I like to spend time with."

"I've said I'll apologise. What more can I do?"

Lauren found a bench and sat down. "I don't know that I can trust your promises."

"Lauren, please, you know I love you," Josh sounded genuinely penitent. "You mean the world to me. Can't you at least try to see things from my point of view?"

"Josh, you pushed Zak into the kitchen table, and you were rude to Pritvia."

"I can't do this over the phone, Lauren. You said you'd come over tonight."

"That was before."

"Please, Lauren. Come round after work. I'll cook something, or we can get a takeaway. I just want to explain things properly."

Lauren still wasn't convinced. "I need time to think."

Josh knew he had to turn the screw.

"This is the first day in my own place, Lauren. I can make things right if you let me. Come at seven, yeah?"

Lauren could feel her heartstrings pull at his pitiful request. There was so much to like and love about Josh that she couldn't bring herself to push him away despite her nagging reservations. The good still held sway over the bad.

"All right," she said. "I'll come."

22

He'd clearly made the effort. Lauren wasn't entirely sure what to expect when Josh opened the door, but she was pleasantly surprised at how tidy the place was. There were no bin liners full of clothes still to put away, and such ornaments and personal effects that he had were all neatly in place. She noticed he'd set the kitchen table for two. A bottle of non-alcoholic wine was placed in the centre beside a couple of candles. She could smell something cooking in the oven.

"I hope you're hungry," Josh said, ushering Lauren into the living room. "It's pasta bake."

He'd made an extra effort with his appearance too. Although wearing one of his favoured checked shirts and immaculate dark trousers, he'd had his hair cut a little shorter than usual and Lauren thought that it suited him. Lauren by comparison was underdressed in her jeans and tee shirt. Josh didn't seem to mind.

"It'll be ready in twenty minutes. You can sit down if you like." He motioned for her to sit on the sofa. "Do you want a drink? There's non-alcoholic Sauvignon Blanc, if you want to try some."

Lauren had hardly said a word since she'd arrived and found it an effort to sound enthusiastic.

"Thank you," she said quietly. Josh brought her a glass.

"I've no idea what this stuff tastes like," he said, pouring himself a glass. "Let's educate ourselves shall we? Here's to happy times. Cheers!" They sipped the wine. Josh pulled a face.

"A bit sweet."

Lauren offered no opinion. She dug into her bag and handed Josh a blue envelope.

"This is for you," she said.

He opened it. It was a simple 'welcome to your new home' card. It was the only one he'd received. Lauren had written, 'all my love' on the inside. She'd bought the card last week and had considered not giving it to him in light of Sunday, but in the end she thought it would be petty not to.

"Thanks," Josh said. He placed it on the mantelpiece and turned back to her. She was biting her lip and looking down into her wine. "I want us to be friends again, Lauren," he said, the regret evident in his voice. Lauren still said nothing.

"How can I make things right?" He came across and knelt in front of her, taking her hand. "Whatever you want me to do, I'll do it. Just tell me."

Lauren could feel her eyes prickle as she fought to check her tears. She was still raw from everything that had happened yesterday and was struggling to think straight.

"Do I really need to tell you?" she said, her lips beginning to quiver. She bit down hard again in an attempt to gain some measure of control.

Josh wiped a single teardrop from her cheek. "There's been enough of those, Lauren. I promise you; everything will be different from now on." He waited for her response, but she was clearly trying to choke back her tears to be able to say anything.

"Lauren, I love you so much." He was welling up himself now. "You're the best thing that's happened to me. The thought that…"

She could hold back no longer, and the tears came. He wanted to embrace her, his soul ached to give her the comfort she needed, but he held back, scared she'd reject him.

"I need to check the oven," he said and left her to her tears. When he came back she'd gathered herself and was on her feet.

"You feeling better, yeah?"

She nodded and sniffed. "Can I help with anything?"

Josh said, "Job's done. Food's ready when you are."

They went into the kitchen and Josh lit the candles. He pulled out a chair for Lauren. She smiled weakly. "I'm sorry for crying," she said, sitting down. "It wasn't just about you… us."

Josh looked relieved. "Your gran? I thought you two made up."

"We have. It's just that I still can't believe she hit me. And with you and Zak on top of everything else…"

Josh lifted the bake out of the oven. "Cross my heart, Lauren, it'll never happen again."

She sipped her drink. "You'd like him if you got to know him."

"Well I've pissed out that bonfire good and proper. Besides, it's probably better if I'm not around when you see him." He started to spoon out the pasta. "Is that too much?" he asked showing her the helping.

"That's fine thank you."

He handed over the plate, ladled a portion for himself and then joined Lauren at the table. She raised her glass.

"To your new home," she said, still a little sniffily. They touched glasses.

"A new start, in more ways than one," Josh said, grinning at last.

Lauren dug into her pasta. It was gorgeous.

"I don't suppose you've heard anything from your mum and dad."

Josh shook his head. "No. They were at work when I went round for my stuff."

"I can't believe how they're acting. I mean, not to support you."

"They never have supported me, really."

"I don't understand why."

"I've already said. I was an accident, an inconvenience."

Lauren was full of sympathy for him again. It was little wonder the lad was mixed up emotionally.

"Maybe you should talk to someone about it. A counsellor."

"I'd rather just forget about it."

"But you haven't forgotten it have you? Josh, what your dad has said to you and what he's done, it's all so wrong. I mean, actually hitting you. It's abuse."

"And so's giving someone a slap across the face. He's still my dad, Lauren."

His words shook her. Yes, the slap from her gran was abuse, and there had been no justification for it.

"Lauren, what matters is you and me," he continued. "That's all I care about. I know I got it wrong yesterday, but you're all I really have."

So much was beginning to make sense to Lauren now. Here was a lad, desperate for love and affection and anything that threatened the tenderness he'd been so short of in his life put him on the attack. She took his hand and squeezed it.

23

Josh's situation and revelations of the past brought into sharp focus the recent behaviour of Lauren's grandparents. Unlike Josh though, she didn't doubt their love, but then, she'd generally complied with their wishes all of her life. Of course, there'd been the odd falling out now and again, the usual kids and teenagers' stuff, nothing serious, but her birthday was a different matter. Her gran had slapped her across the cheek for no excusable reason that she could think of. (Lauren had only raised her voice in self-defence after all.) And then there was the 'fatherly advice' given to Josh a few days beforehand. She was determined to press them on these matters as soon as she could, maybe then she'd understand Josh's parents a bit more and make better sense of things.

What if I were to start rocking the boat and make decisions that they weren't happy about, she wondered? *How would they react then? Like Josh's mum and dad?*

"You're very quiet, Lauren," Geoff remarked as they all sat at the dining table with their evening meal. "Is everything all right?"

Lauren pushed some carrots around her plate with little enthusiasm, trying to pluck up the courage to challenge them both. She knew she'd have to be careful, this wasn't a witch-hunt and the last thing she wanted was a row.

"I'm not very hungry," she said.

"Are you ill?"

"There's a few thing's on my mind that's all."

"Something to do with Josh?" Iris ventured.

"Partly."

"You've not fallen out?"

Lauren shook her head. She wanted to tell them about Josh and how his dad used to hit him to give some kind of context to what she was dying to get off her chest. "Josh told me that you had a word with him last week," Lauren said, hesitantly.

Geoff chewed his food slowly and swallowed. "Oh yes?"

"Why?"

"I'm just looking out for you, that's all."

"Don't you think I can look out for myself?" Lauren said, sounding put out. "I'm twenty and you've no right—"

"I'm your grandad, I've every right." He was firm, and Lauren knew she was already standing on thin ice. She backed off and looked down at her plate, feeling the warm rush of blood in her cheeks.

"Given half a chance he'll push you faster than you want to go," he added more softly. "I'm not saying he isn't a decent lad, but I just want you to be careful."

Lauren toyed with a chunk of chicken that she'd no intention of eating.

"His dad used to hit him," she said wondering if she was doing the right thing by finally broadcasting the news. "He's had it a bit hard at home."

Iris frowned. "I thought you said his parents were nice."

Lauren explained Josh's past situation as best she could remember it. When she'd finished, Geoff said,

"Explains why he's got a bit of edge, I suppose."

"It's horrible," Lauren said. "They never let him forget he was an accident."

"Well, it's very sad, but it is at it is, Lauren, " Iris said. "And that means you have to be especially careful where he's concerned. You haven't had to fight for anything like he obviously has, especially for affection, and that's why you have a gentle nature. You could easily be taken advantage of."

There was certainly truth in her gran's words, but Lauren hadn't finished yet. "Why did you hit me?"

The question was a bombshell and Lauren could clearly see the colour drain from her gran's face.

"I thought that matter was closed," she said.

"I just want to understand why you did it." Lauren was desperate not to sound aggressive, but she wanted the answer.

"Lauren, I'll regret what I did for the rest of my life. I don't know what came over me, I really don't."

"Have you felt like hitting me before?"

"Lauren, what is this, stop it please!"

Geoff intervened. "You've gone far enough, Lauren. What's got into you? I don't want any mention of this subject again, do you hear?"

Lauren was looking down at her plate again, biting her lip. She made no response.

"I asked you a question, Lauren; did you hear?"

"Yes," she said, curtly.

There was a long silence. Appetites quickly waned. When Lauren had had enough of the awkward atmosphere, she announced that she was going up to her room, grateful at least that a major argument hadn't ensued. She hadn't been there long when her grandad knocked on the door.

"Can I come in?"

Lauren got off her bed and opened the door. She could see concern on his face rather than anger. He sat beside her on the bed.

"You've upset your gran."

Lauren messed with her watchstrap. "I know," she said sheepishly.

"I'm not too chuffed myself."

Lauren nodded.

"So what's going on?" Geoff pressed.

She thought long and hard before saying anything. "I'm trying to make sense of what's happened to Josh," she said eventually. "I just thought that...well..."

"We're not Josh's parents," Geoff said as her voice tailed off. "Your gran and me have always put your well-being and happiness first. You know that. Our job is to love

109

and worry about you, but I'm not going to apologise for trying to protect you. I'll do that until my dying day."

Lauren was quiet again. Geoff continued:

"We're also human beings and we make mistakes. Your gran knows that she was wrong to do what she did. Happen she was stressed with all the preparation for your party, I don't know. It's not often you answer either of us back and maybe you caught her at a bad time. She hasn't forgiven herself and I don't want you throwing it at her every time you have a difference."

"I'm not going to."

"You need to apologise."

"I will."

There was another pause. Geoff took Lauren's hand.

"You have to understand that your gran and me still see you as our little girl. The reality is that you're a young woman growing up faster than we'd like. It won't be too long before you fly the nest, and that prospect is hard for us."

"I'm sorry," she said. "I wasn't meaning to get at you both, it's just that—"

"It's all right, Lauren," Geoff cut in quickly as if he didn't want to hear her explanation. "I understand. Now come on downstairs and let's fix things with your gran."

24

S he quickened her step. Although she could no longer see the middle-aged man, she knew he was still following. At each aisle end he seemed to be there, checking his phone or pretending to be interested in picking something from the shelves even though she'd caught him looking at her enough times to dismiss coincidence. It wasn't the biggest Co-op in the world, you saw the same faces almost every day, but one face Lauren didn't want to see was *his*. She'd still a few more items to get and half considered calling it a day, but she'd promised Josh she'd get them a deluxe pizza, nibbles and non-alcoholic wine. (He was still keeping his promise to lay off the hard stuff.) When she got to the wine counter her peripheral vision picked out the man loitering a few yards away. She quickly grabbed a bottle of zero-alcohol pinot, dumped it into her basket and tried to think if she'd forgotten anything. There were still the mixed nuts and cake bars to get. If she got her skates on she'd be out of the place in a couple of minutes. As she headed for the cakes, she flipped her phone onto selfie mode and held it so she could see over her shoulder without turning round.

I shouldn't have to do this, she thought to herself, taking a quick turn onto the confectionery aisle. She scanned the shelves, found the nuts and then went to the cakes, all the time checking her phone screen. She didn't doubt herself, not any more. The rationale she'd used previously to dismiss the man's presence was no longer holding water, particularly after Saturday morning when he'd been in the same café in town. Coincidence was a word she was no longer prepared to accept. She was now beginning to feel seriously creeped out by the man.

The cakes were just around the corner, and she grabbed some lemon drizzle bars before going over to the checkout. She unloaded her goods and reached into her bag for her purse. She glanced to her left and saw that the man was next in line. He'd two items in his hand; he could have used the self-service tills. Lauren raised her phone to her ear, masking the fact that it was still on selfie mode and angled it so that the man would be in shot. She pressed the shutter button, hoping she'd hit the bullseye. Minutes later she was back at her car scrutinising the image she'd covertly managed to take. It was a little bit blurry, but there was no doubt that the man was looking at her in a way that she didn't think was natural. She could feel the heavy beat of her heart and she knew she couldn't stay silent any longer. She was loath to tell her grandparents because they'd inevitably kick up a stink and want to drag the police into things. Besides, apart from the blurred photo, she couldn't prove anything. She'd run it past Josh first.

"Why didn't you say something sooner?" Josh said, enlarging the image on her phone. "You hear all sorts of things these days."

"I've only just been sure," Lauren said. "I can't just go around accusing people of stalking." She'd unpacked the shopping, which was now piled on Josh's kitchen table before hitting him with the news.

"Has he ever approached you, said anything?" he asked.

"No. He just stares, and I think he's been taking pictures."

"You know you'll have to report him."

"I don't think I can prove anything."

"Well you can't live your life looking over your shoulder the whole time. He might be dangerous, the weird bastard. Do you know anything about him? Where he might live, what car he drives?"

"He has a silver one; I can't remember what make it is. And I think he's married or has a partner."

Josh ran his hands through his hair. "You've got me worried now, Lauren. You should have told me sooner." He noticed she was biting her lip. "They've got cameras at the Co-op haven't they?"

"I think so."

"Well it'll be a cinch for the cops to nail him then."

Lauren looked decidedly uncomfortable. Her doubts were creeping back again.

"Josh, I'd rather not. Not yet anyway. If I'm wrong…"

"You just said you were sure."

113

"I know."

Josh thought for a moment. "Well, if we want to be absolutely certain, we'll have to do a bit of our own detective work, won't we?"

"How do you mean?"

"For starters, I can be around when you get off the train. I can keep my eyes on him and see if he really is gawping at you. I could follow him home, at least we'd find out where he lives."

Lauren was far from convinced. "I don't like that idea."

"So go to the police."

Lauren pulled a face. "I need to think about things. Maybe if I got some more photos."

"You're kidding aren't you? And it's risky. This bloke might be a nutcase. What if he sees you snapping away?"

"I don't know."

Josh took Lauren's hands in his. "Let's do this my way. Just to make sure."

25

The plan was straightforward. Lauren was to message Josh the moment she saw the middle-aged man on the train. Josh would then drive to Fitzwilliam station and watch for the man, observe his actions and take note of the car he drove. He would then carefully follow the man to see whether he tailed Lauren or went straight home. Josh had been waiting anxiously for her text from around five and eventually received her message at half past. He'd only finished work fifteen minutes ago, and it was going to be a rush to get to the station in time for the train. He was a good driver, knew which rat runs to take so he could avoid the speed cameras and where he could take calculated risks with the traffic flow. Employing his wits, and occasionally incurring the wrath of other motorists, he managed to get to Fitzwilliam with three minutes to spare. There was no room in the car park, so he pulled outside a row of terrace houses that faced the main station steps and waited. He could hear the train arrive and the beeping of the doors as they opened. He saw Lauren emerge from the steps and make purposefully for her car. A moment later he spotted the middle-aged man closely following. Josh recorded the man on his phone and noticed that he was clearly looking at her.

He cursed and watched as the man then sauntered over to his silver Volkswagen, parked on the same row as Lauren. The bastard would have parked next to her if he could. Josh photographed the number plate and fired up his engine as he saw Lauren drive away. The Volkswagen duly followed. Josh moved away in pursuit.

Lauren followed her usual route home, the Volkswagen staying with her most of the way. When she branched off left down a small side road, the Volkswagen seemed to hesitate, as if considering whether to follow. In the end it continued on ahead. Josh stayed close. The Volkswagen picked up speed and looked initially to be making for Pontefract. Josh allowed a car to overtake him but kept his eye on the Volkswagen. After a half-mile or so, it made a right turn into a large, modern housing estate. The man was obviously quite local. Josh eased off as the Volkswagen made another right turn into a spacious avenue Josh knew as Sycamore Grove. He cruised by as the Volkswagen turned into the wide driveway of a neat, detached stone-built house, squinting to make out the house number. Forty-five.

"Got you," he said softly to himself. He kicked down on the accelerator and turned for home.

26

The images in isolation didn't really prove very much. They were certainly nothing you could hang a man by, so Josh suggested that they continued their surveillance for a further week, gathering more evidence, but Lauren was far from happy.

"We might end up getting into trouble ourselves," she said. They were at Josh's flat huddled on the sofa, finishing the last of the non-alcoholic pinot Lauren had brought yesterday.

"We just need one image, one video that can prove that he's following you," Josh countered. "Maybe you could drop in at the Co-op instead of going straight home. See if he takes the bait."

Lauren could scarcely believe this was happening to her. "I wish I'd never started this."

"We can't stop now."

Lauren's head was spinning. "I'll see if I can get close to him on the train and have my phone ready if he tries anything. I don't want you following him, Josh. We have his car number, we know where he lives, let's just keep it at that for the moment."

She knew that once they got their evidence, involving the police was inevitable. The thought made her shudder, as did the prospect of finally telling her grandparents. She desperately hoped she'd got all of this wrong, but she was cutting against her intuition, which was screaming like a banshee at her.

"If that's how you want it," Josh said, though something in his expression suggested he might have other ideas.

27

At first when she saw the bunch of flowers attached to the windscreen of her car she thought they were a surprise gift from Josh. However, the card that accompanied them had no message other than two kisses drawn in black ink. Besides, flowers weren't Josh's style. . Nevertheless, she checked with him all the same. No, he hadn't sent them, but he could guess who had. She removed the flowers; chrysanthemums and carnations, a riotous mix of vivid colours that under normal circumstances would have delighted her and put them in her car. She looked around the car park for the middle-aged man. She hadn't seen him either at Leeds or on the train today. If her suspicions were correct, that he was the person behind the gift, then he must have made a special trip. If things weren't scary enough, they certainly were now. But she had no proof that the man had given her the flowers, though she supposed that the station's CCTV might have picked something up. Perhaps now was the time to go to the police. She mulled things over as she drove home. When she arrived, she thought about dumping the flowers in the bin, but they were evidence. For now, she'd have to pass them off as a gift from Josh. She knew that having the flowers on display would be a constant reminder that she was being stalked, but it couldn't be helped. To add to her misery, her gran put them centre stage on the living room table, cooing how beautiful they were.

It had just passed six o'clock when Lauren's phone beeped a message from Josh. He was running late. Could she come over at half past eight rather than seven tonight? It was unusual for him to run late on a Friday, but sometimes a late evening avoided the need to work on a Saturday morning. Perhaps this was one of those times. She packed her overnight bag, and then had a shower, her mind fixated on the flowers and the fact that things had now escalated. Why would the man send her flowers? As a token of his affection, perhaps? That thought made her shudder. He was certainly becoming braver. Would he eventually approach her? Try to speak to her? She couldn't hold off for much longer. She was going to have to tell her grandparents over the weekend about what was going on.

She messaged Josh to let him know she was on her way. He'd said they would go out for a bite to eat, and given what had happened today, she was looking forward to it. Usually he acknowledged quite quickly, but he'd made no response by the time she arrived. Although it wasn't yet dark, the light was beginning to fade, and there were a few lights dotted here and there, but Josh's flat looked dead. His car wasn't anywhere in sight, either. Perhaps he was still at the garage, or maybe he'd broken down and he was on the bus or even walking home. But if that were the case, surely he'd have phoned? Lauren got out of her car and went up to the main entrance just in case he was home, rang the bell and waited. No response. She tried a couple more times, but he clearly wasn't in. She checked her phone. Nothing. She called his mobile, but it was turned off, then the garage but there was no answer. Lauren was mystified and went back to her car feeling slightly worried. *I'll give him ten minutes,* she thought and checked her phone again. It rang five minutes later. Lauren saw that it was her gran, and her heart sank.

"Hi, Gran," she said, hardly masking her disappointment.

"Lauren where are you?" Her gran sounded anxious.

"I'm over at Josh's waiting for him to come home, he's running late, why?"

"The police are here; they want to have a word with you about something."

"The police?" Lauren's heart gave a jolt. "Nothing's happened to Josh has it?" There was no hiding the alarm in her voice.

"Just come home, Lauren."

"What's happened?"

"I don't know, just get yourself home!" The line went dead.

Lauren bit on her lip; her mouth ran as dry as the desert. She started her car with a trembling hand, her mind a sea of worried thoughts. *Something must have happened to Josh,* she thought, trying to steady her nerves. She kicked down on the accelerator and headed quickly home.

28

Lauren had never been blessed with the rosiest of complexions, but even by her standards her face was ghostly white. Her large brown eyes were full of concern and uncertainty as she came into the living room. Iris, equally ashen-faced, was sitting on the sofa. Geoff was in his favourite armchair, a worried look etched across his face.

"What's going on?" Lauren asked, sliding her bag from her shoulder. The sight of a policeman standing in the living room unnerved her; her trembling body seemed to have a mind of its own.

"This gentleman would like to have a word with you," Geoff said, grimly.

The police 'gentleman' introduced himself as PC Raven. He was probably in his thirties, Lauren surmised, and quite tall, his height accentuated by his slender frame. His radio crackled every now and again, puncturing the tense atmosphere with so much static that it could have exploded.

Lauren sat next to her gran, her breathing shallow against the nervous palpitations of her heart.

"This is a bit complicated," PC Raven said, hesitantly. "So we'll start with first things first. Can I confirm that you are Miss Lauren Melissa Wright?"

Lauren nodded.

"And this is your permanent address?"

Another nod.

"Can you confirm your age please?"

"Twenty."

Raven seemed satisfied. "Can you confirm that you are acquainted with a Mr Joshua Armstrong of…?"

"I'm his girlfriend," Lauren said impatiently. "What's happened to him?" She grabbed her gran's hand and squeezed it, bracing herself for terrible news.

"We have him down at the station. He's got himself into a bit of trouble."

Lauren frowned. "What kind of trouble?"

"This evening, Joshua Armstrong allegedly attacked and committed grievous bodily harm to a Mr Leonard Thomas outside his home of forty-five Sycamore Grove. Does anything ring a bell, miss?"

Lauren was stunned into silence at this revelation. What vestige of colour that had been on her face evaporated completely. The same vapid pallor washed over the countenances of both Iris and Geoff.

"No," Iris croaked hoarsely. "That can't be true."

"There were witnesses Mrs Wright. I can assure you that it happened."

"Dear God," Iris said, her voice barely a whisper.

Lauren frowned as the victim's name echoed and rebounded in her brain.

"Leonard Thomas? That's the same name as my dad," she said. "It's a funny coincidence."

"There's nothing coincidental about it, Miss Wright," Raven said.

"What do you mean?"

Raven cleared his throat. "First things first, Miss Wright. According to your boyfriend, you claim that Leonard Thomas was following you. Stalking might be a better way of putting it."

"Jesus Christ," Geoff said. "This is getting worse."

"A man was watching me, yes," Lauren said, aware that her grandparents were horribly quiet, "but I still don't know what you mean about nothing being coincidental."

"I'll come to that in just a moment," Raven said, ignoring the static that once more emitted from his radio. "Your boyfriend says he was acting in your defence, that this man was making your life a misery."

Lauren's eyes were beginning to sting with tears. She squeezed her gran's hand, seeking comfort and turned to her. "I'm sorry, I should have told you about this. I've got this all wrong." She tried to supress her sobs.

"*Was* he making your life a misery?" Raven pressed.

Lauren took a few moments to compose herself. "I've caught him watching me lots of times, mainly on the train, but I'd see him sometimes at the Co-op round the corner, messing around with his phone, like he was taking photos of me but trying to hide it at the same time. Josh wanted me to go to the police, but I couldn't prove anything, so we had the idea of getting our own evidence. Josh followed him from the station to track his movements, but I didn't know he was going to do something like this."

"And you didn't once recognise that this man was your father?"

"What are you talking about? My dad's dead."

"No, Miss Wright," Raven said. "Leonard Thomas might be battered and bruised at the moment, but he's still very much alive."

"Dad was killed in a car accident," Lauren insisted. "I've never seen him. Tell him, Gran."

Raven felt as if he were standing in quicksand. This was an issue outside of his jurisdiction as well as his understanding. The last thing he wanted was to get involved in family politics. His job was to piece together the motive behind Josh's attack on Thomas and what part Lauren played in it, nothing else.

"I think there are things you all need to discuss," Raven said tactfully. "I do assure you Miss Wright that our information is correct. I can see that you're shocked, so I think it would be better to arrange a visit at another time, all things considered. At this stage it's nothing official and from what we've learned from Mr Armstrong it's highly unlikely you'd be charged with anything. We're looking at tomorrow afternoon, depending on our workload. Failing that, you'll be informed to come down to the station."

Lauren stared blankly back at him.

"I'm sorry for the shock, Miss Wright." Raven bade a hasty goodnight and saw himself out of the house.

They sat in silence for what seemed a year. Iris and Geoff were stunned that the secret they had held for so long had now escaped like some beast from hell. On top of this, they were appalled by the fact that their son-in-law had apparently been stalking Lauren without any intimation from her that anything was wrong. Geoff got up from his seat looking like a man facing the gallows, knowing that whatever he said couldn't repair the damage done, but he tried anyway.

"Lauren," he said, his voice gruff, broken. "You have to understand that there are reasons why we told you that your dad was dead."

Lauren wasn't listening. "My dad's *alive* and you knew all the time," she said, struggling to comprehend the bombshell that had blown her world apart. "You've been lying to me all of my life. How could you?"

Iris rested a tentative hand on Lauren's shoulder, but she shrugged it off.

"Don't touch me," Lauren spat. "Don't even speak to me." She got up from the sofa, grabbed her bag and car keys and made for the door.

"Lauren where are you going?" Iris called. "Lauren, we need to talk!"

The only response was the sound of the front door being slammed.

Lauren got into her car, started the engine and drove away. She didn't know where she was heading just so long as it was away from home, whatever that word meant now. When she'd been driving for little more than five minutes, she pulled into the roadside, got out her phone and called Pritvia. She was always a good listener and had a practical head on her shoulders; she'd surely be able to offer some solace or advice to help her get her head round things. She scrolled through her phone contacts, found her number and punched the call button. She was shaking as she waited for her friend to answer, a fervid cocktail of anger, confusion and nervous exhaustion washing over her like a great tsunami. When her friend answered, Lauren struggled to get any coherent words out of her parched mouth. "Pritvia, hi… erm… I… I was wondering if… if I could come over?" She was taking breaths, desperately trying to hold herself together.

Pritvia was immediately concerned for her friend.

"Lauren, what's happened? Where are you? Are you hurt?"

"I-I'm in my car," Lauren said, crying a little more openly now.

"Of course you can come over," Pritvia said. "You don't sound as if you're in good shape. Are you sure you should be driving?"

"I'll be all right," Lauren sniffed. "I'll see you in about half an hour."

"For God's sake Lauren, please be careful. Should I come over to you?"

"No," Lauren said emphatically. "I-I'm on my way."

Pritvia's home was in Colton, six miles east of Leeds city centre and was a relatively straightforward journey, which was just as well as Lauren was functioning on auto pilot for most of the trip. She could hear her phone vibrating and pinging on the seat beside her as she drove. She knew it would be her grandparents trying to get in touch, but to hell with them. As soon as she got to Pritvia's she'd turn the damned thing off. It was almost dark, and Lauren was finding it a strain to drive through her tear-streaked eyes and the glare of lights as traffic flashed by. She wiped her running nose on her sleeve as the enormity of the evening's revelations pummelled her brain. As her mind wandered, she almost took a wrong turn and swung back into lane without properly checking her mirror, incurring the wrath of several cars behind her who had to take evasive action. Raising an apologetic hand, she tried to gather her concentration, but it was hopelessly fragmented, and it continually showed in her erratic driving. When she finally arrived at her friend's it was a wonder she hadn't been involved in some sort of incident.

Pritvia was waiting in the spacious driveway as Lauren pulled in alongside the black Mazda parked there. When she got out of her car, Pritvia greeted her with an expression of concern on her face.

"My God Lauren, you look a mess." She took her friend's hands in hers. "What's happened to you?"

Lauren knew that she wouldn't be able to contain the

flood of emotions waiting to burst through the walls of her rapidly waning willpower and managed to say, "Help me, please," before they erupted.

29

Lauren had only met Pritvia's parents once before, when she'd been to Pritvia's twenty-first birthday party, a full-on family affair held at the Dhawan's house. Although that happy occasion was only six months ago, it seemed a lifetime away now. A good-looking couple in their late forties, the Dhawan's oozed middle-class opulence. Pritvia's mum, Reeva was as flamboyant in her choice of dress as was her daughter, favouring vivid colour clashes that were reminiscent of the psychedelic age of the 1960s. Her electric blue dress glared against the livid red of her tights, and in contrast to them both, Ganesh, Pritvia's dad, wore a simple white shirt and black trousers. Pritvia's younger brother, Rupesh, a wily thirteen-year-old, was happy in his LA Lakers tee shirt and jeans. They were all watching the television when Pritvia brought Lauren through into the lounge. They could see she was looking washed out and had been crying, and acknowledged her thin, brave smile respectfully. Pritvia had warned them that something wasn't right after she'd told them Lauren was calling round so they weren't overly surprised by the girl's fragile appearance.

"We're just going up to my room," Pritvia said.

"Of course," Ganesh said in a voice that exuded compassion even though he'd no idea what Lauren's problem was and was far too polite to ask. "Would either of you like a drink? Tea, coffee?"

Lauren shook her head. "No thank you," she said softly. If she drank or ate anything at the moment it would probably end up being heaved onto the carpet.

Pritvia took Lauren up to her room. At any other time Lauren would have taken more notice of her surroundings, but as it was, everything was a haze. They sat on the bed, Lauren immediately burying her head in her hands. Pritvia placed a comforting arm around Lauren's shoulders and kissed her forehead. As blunt as she could be with Lauren at times, this moment of tenderness was quite simply bathed in love for her friend.

"I don't know where to start," Lauren sobbed as mascara stained tears trickled down her cheeks. Pritvia handed her a tissue. Lauren blew her nose and tried to explain the evening's events in some way that might make sense to her friend. Pritvia listened in utter disbelief as her friend struggled to tell her of how she suspected she was being stalked, and how she had wanted to get more evidence so that she could go confidently to the police to make a complaint. When Lauren got to the part about Josh being arrested, she broke down again. However, Pritvia's earlier disbelief was as nothing compared to what followed.

"The man who Josh beat up was my dad." Lauren's voice was barely audible as the knot that had been strangling her throat for the past hour threatened to choke her altogether. "They've been lying to me! All this time I thought my dad was dead."

Pritvia was both stunned and appalled. "I don't know what to say," she said, not even trying to conceal her shock. "I mean you couldn't make it up could you? It's bad enough that Josh has been arrested, but this!"

Lauren continued to sob, unable to rationalise anything. So much was coming at her. The prospect of further questions by the police, Josh's arrest and a dad now back from the dead was all the stuff of nightmares, but what troubled her more than anything were the lies her grandparents had told her. Why, why, why had they lied?

"I feel as if I don't know them any more," Lauren said, wiping her nose on another tissue. "Or that I can ever trust them again. I just can't believe that Dad's alive and they knew all along."

"I think we have to deal with first things first," Pritvia said, running a hand through her hair, not entirely sure what the first thing might be. "Are you intending to go home tonight?"

Lauren shrugged. "I don't know."

"I can ask Mum and Dad if you can stay over," Pritvia said synchronously reflecting what had happened to Josh when he'd fallen out with his parents not so long ago.

"Thank you," Lauren said faintly. "Tell me what do, Pritvia."

"Oh, God, Lauren I don't know," Pritvia said feeling wretched and powerless. "I don't suppose we can really do anything until morning. Maybe when you've had some rest things might be a bit clearer."

"I feel like I've been an idiot all of my life."

"You could never be that." Pritvia was quick to challenge her friend's self-deprecating remark. "If you can't trust your own family to tell you the truth about things, who can you trust?"

"There's so much I don't understand. Why did Dad leave, and why has he come back now? And then there's Josh and the mess he's in; God, I just can't get my head round any of it."

"Neither can I," Pritvia said. "I'm going to have to put Mum and Dad in the picture, if you don't mind. They'll be fine about you staying over, trust me. Let's look at this in the morning; my head's a shed, so what yours must be like I can only imagine."

Lauren was given the spare room. It was small and looked like it was hardly ever used. The single bed was softer than Lauren was used to, she felt as if it wanted to console her, draw her into itself and soothe away her worries, or maybe it wanted to suck her down into the depths of itself, to suffocate her and draw a black veil over her eyes shutting out all light, leaving her to sink into blissful oblivion. The way she felt at the moment, she didn't particularly care which. Sleep was as far from her as the distant stars though, so she checked her phone knowing there'd be a string of messages and missed calls to wade through. Her gran had tried to call seven times, she noticed, and she'd texted a further twelve. The last message was the only one Lauren was interested in responding to. *Please let us know that you're all right.* Lauren punched her reply: *I'm staying with a friend. I don't know when I'll be back*, and promptly shut off her phone. She pulled the covers over her head and closed her eyes.

At seven a.m., she awoke and for a moment hadn't a clue where she was. She hadn't slept well and to make things worse she had a thumping headache. Desperate for a pee and feeling light-headed, she padded along the landing and made for the toilet. She could hear the television downstairs; the muffled sound of explosions and gunfire were ringing out a bit too loudly for this time in the morning. Rupesh was probably playing on his X-box. She squatted on the toilet and tried to gather her thoughts as the heavy weight of circumstances pressed down on her like an iron fist. She knew she would have to go home today and face her grandparents, but her anger and sense of betrayal hadn't yet subsided. Besides, she had to be around home for when the police got in touch. There would be no resolution to the storm of questions that raged through her brain unless she had it out with them, but the thought of confrontation turned her stomach. She was a long way from forgiving them, if she ever could. But there was also the matter of Josh to consider. She could only guess at the trouble he was in. GBH was serious, but what sort of punishment it carried she had no idea. Maybe she'd google the answer later. And then there was her dad; the dead man who'd wanted nothing to do with her all her life until now. The man who'd been stalking her, watching her movements, scaring her from the shadows like a ghost. The man who'd caused all this trouble. The man she knew she would eventually have to meet.

She freshened herself up, looked in the mirror and saw a bedraggled mess staring back at her. *My God,* she thought. *I look ninety.* Her eyes were bloodshot and swollen and there still wasn't a trace of colour in her cheeks. She combed her fingers through her tangled hair, making the best of a bad job.

Not wanting to disturb anyone, she went back to her room and turned on her phone. Once it came to life, it alerted her to endless messages from her grandparents but there was nothing at all from Josh. She googled the likely punishment for GBH and was astounded to find that it carried a lengthy custodial sentence. *This is my fault,* she thought to herself, guiltily. *If I'd gone to the police sooner Josh would never have been arrested.* She cursed her weakness and wished she'd faced things head on; however, regardless of her own failings and Josh's actions, it didn't alter the fact that her dad was on the scene. At what point he would have formally announced his presence she'd only know by asking him.

A further half hour passed before Lauren heard her hosts show further signs of stirring. Someone was going downstairs, there was an exchange of voices and the volume of the TV dropped. Moments later, the kettle clicked on. There was a faint tapping on Lauren's door.

"Are you awake?" Pritvia said from the other side.

Lauren opened the door to her friend who looked unbelievably stunning in her white nightie.

"My eyes are open, I'm not sure about the rest of me," she said.

"Brain still addled?"

"You could say that."

"Want some breakfast?"

Lauren shook her head.

"I'll have a coffee if there's one going."

"Sure. Are you coming down for it, or do you want it in here?"

"I have to face the world some time," Lauren said. "I'll come down."

"Do you want twenty minutes to look human first?"

Lauren smiled bravely.

"Give me three days and I might just get there."

When Lauren went downstairs she looked a sight better than she had done an hour ago. She couldn't do much about her puffy eyes, but she'd dabbed a bit of colour onto her cheeks and added some mascara to her eyes, so she no longer looked like a corpse. Rupesh, engrossed in his war game, hardly acknowledged her as she trudged into the living room and through into the adjoining kitchen. The smell of strong coffee and pancakes hit her like an oncoming train. Pritvia, no longer in her nightie, was distinctively dressed to attract attention. Her orange dress, matched with similarly coloured glasses, was tied at the waist with a blue belt that had a large white buckle. The plimsolls on her feet were a mixture of white and lime-green swirls. She was in many ways noisier than the game Rupesh was playing on the X-box, but the riot of colour was merely a reflection of the vivacious and incredibly warm person Lauren loved so much. Nevertheless, the vibrancy of Pritvia's clothes did little to aid Lauren's thick head. Ganesh was in his burgundy nightgown, reaching for a tin of treacle from the cupboard. Everyone exchanged pleasantries before Lauren sat at the dining table with her coffee. She took a sip, shuddering at the bitter flavour that danced on her tongue. At least I'm still alive, she thought to herself, hoping the caffeine would kick in quickly.

"Any clearer how you're going to play it today?" Pritvia said, sitting opposite Lauren and munching a pancake.

"Putting first things first; home I suppose," Lauren said.

"Have you worked out what you're going to say?"

Lauren shook her head. "The more I think about it the angrier I get. I'll just wing it I guess."

"Yes, over-thinking's a bit of a pain," Pritvia agreed.

Ganesh joined them at the table with his pancakes. Although Lauren's personal life wasn't really any of his business, the fact that the girl was sitting directly in front of him because of it gave him some leave to comment.

"Tread slowly and carefully, love," he said. "At the moment I'm sure you have lots of questions. Until you get some answers you can't know what to do or what to say. Let your grandparents explain themselves, then you'll be in a better place to make any judgement."

Lauren bit down on her lip and smiled thinly at the well-meaning advice.

"I'm dreading it," she said faintly.

Lauren drove slowly home. Feelings of nausea washed over her as the roads got more familiar the closer she got to home. Her heart raced and her mouth was bone dry as she turned into the driveway and parked behind her grandad's BMW. It was strange how your own home could fill you with so much apprehension. She got out of her car and walked over to the front door, taking some steadying breaths to check her thundering heart. Stepping into the hallway she was met with the gush of familiar, homely smells. She noticed one of her jackets on the hook near the hallway mirror, and several pairs of her shoes by the radiator. Everything seemed so normal.

At the sound of Lauren's return, the living room door opened. Her gran was standing directly in front of her and looked shocking.

"Lauren, thank God," she said, her voice sounded hoarse. She'd clearly been doing a lot of crying. If her voice hadn't given her away, her drawn, blanched complexion certainly did. Lauren fought hard not to cry herself and focused instead on the anger she felt in an attempt to keep her softer emotions at bay. Before she could say anything, she heard her grandad coming down the stairs. Like her gran, he looked washed out and tired. The white bristles on his chin aged him a good ten years.

"We've been frantic with worry," he said.

"I told you I was staying at a friend's," Lauren replied, careful not to sound too much on the back foot.

"We didn't know when you'd be coming back," Iris said.

"I couldn't stay away very long could I?" Lauren said irritably. "There's too much mess to sort out."

Iris took the retort on the chin. "You look tired. Have you had anything to eat?"

"I'm not hungry."

"A drink then?"

Lauren shook her head.

"Can we just get on with things please?"

They all went through into the living room. Lauren deliberately sat in the armchair closest to the television rather than in her favourite space on the sofa. Iris sat in the opposite armchair. Geoff remained standing, hands dug deeply into his trouser pockets. It was clear that he didn't know how to begin, and all Lauren could do was bite down on her lower lip. Eventually he started, though it was as if he were addressing the floor rather than his granddaughter.

"I know you're angry and confused," he said in a voice Lauren hardly recognised. His usual strength of character seemed to have deserted him. "I probably would be in your shoes, but you have to know that there's a reason why we didn't tell you the truth about your dad."

"You mean there's a reason why you lied," Lauren corrected him without hiding her bitterness.

Geoff nodded. "If that's the way you want to put it." He shuffled uncomfortably on the spot, like a kid explaining bad behaviour to his teacher.

"You see Lauren, your dad isn't a good man. We didn't lie to you about his womanising or affairs. He left your mum before you were born and wanted nothing at all to do with you. Then he got himself into serious trouble." He exchanged an awkward glance with Iris before turning back to Lauren, his eyes meeting hers now. He took a breath. "Your dad was convicted of rape. He did five years. All we know is that once he served his time he moved down to Stevenage. Now it would appear that he's back."

Lauren wasn't sure how many more shocks she could take.

"He raped someone?"

Geoff nodded. "We didn't want you to know the truth. He was dead to us you see, and we wanted you to think the same. You might have had ideas of trying to find him and we didn't want that. We adopted you so you could take our name and told you as little about the man as we could get away with. We were wrong to lie to you, but we thought what good would it do growing up knowing you had a rapist for a dad, especially one who didn't want you. The kids at school would have hammered you for it. So there you have it, the whole shitty gospel truth. Judge us if you like, but we did everything to protect you."

Lauren rubbed her forehead trying to comprehend what she'd just heard.

"We never for a moment thought that he'd come looking for you," Iris said. "I wish you'd told us that you were being followed."

"I didn't want to worry you until I was sure of everything," Lauren said, her tone far more contrite than it had been.

"It's our job to worry and care about you," Iris said; a bit of her old flame returning. "Even if we make mistakes," she added as an afterthought.

Lauren recognised that her grandparents had probably been caught between a rock and a hard place, though she still wasn't happy that they'd lied to her. Perhaps it was more to do with the fact that they'd always been so loving and trustworthy that she'd never thought them capable of deceit; after all, this was a bit bigger than perpetuating the Santa Claus myth.

"Are you all right?" Geoff asked her.

"I don't know," Lauren said, clearly preoccupied. "It's just so unbelievable."

Geoff looked as if a weight had been lifted from his shoulders. He'd at least survived round one without further estranging Lauren.

"We've dreaded this day coming. We hoped you'd never have to find out."

Lauren wanted to cry but she'd shed more tears recently than she had in the last three years and held firm. Regardless of what her dad had done, the man was still alive, and she couldn't help being drawn to him as a flame might lure a moth.

"I'll have to see him," she said, openly. Her grandparents looked crestfallen.

"Lauren, love, you need to think about this carefully," Geoff said. "That man wanted nothing to do with you or your mum. The only person he ever cared about was himself."

"Then he can tell me that to my face."

Iris looked to be on the verge of tears. "Are you spiting us, Lauren?"

Lauren was appalled by the suggestion.

"How could you even think that? We're talking about my dad!"

"A rapist and adulterer!" Iris returned sharply.

Lauren tried to equate the man's crimes with the face she saw on the train. The two didn't match but that didn't mean a thing.

"Gran, he's been following me, and I want to know why! And Josh is in trouble because of him."

Geoff raised a hand calling for calm. "You're right, Lauren," he said. "I'm not happy about what you want to do, but we can't stop you seeing him. The bastard that he is doesn't alter the fact he's your father."

Lauren was quiet for a few moments. "I suppose the police might be able to help with things when I talk to them."

"Maybe," Geoff said. "And what about Josh? Have you thought about what you might do about him?"

"No," Lauren sighed. It was bad enough having a dad who'd served time, but a boyfriend facing the same fate was almost laughable. "I want to get through today first."

"I think that goes for us all, love," Geoff said.

Lauren went her room and flopped wearily onto her bed. She couldn't make her up mind whether or not her grandparents had done the right thing in shielding her from the truth. They'd certainly been convincing liars throughout her life regardless of their good intentions and it bothered her. She sent Pritvia a text saying that she was okay, and she'd get in touch again to put her fully in the picture sometime over the weekend. She wasn't sure if she would be going in to work on Monday though. She also messaged Zak, saying she'd important news for him and she'd call him over the next few days. Messages done, she put her phone on the bedside table and closed her eyes. Within minutes she was fast asleep.

30

"**T**he police are here," Geoff said softly, not wanting to startle Lauren awake.

Lauren opened her eyes; her grandad's features came slowly into focus. She frowned and rubbed her forehead. Her head still ached.

"What?"

"The police are here," Geoff said again.

Lauren's stomach cartwheeled and her heart thumped so hard she could feel the heavy thuds hammer against her chest. She anxiously followed her grandad downstairs and into the living room. It wasn't PC Raven this time but a small female officer who didn't look much older than Lauren. She introduced herself as PC Hamilton and that she was following up the previous visit made by Raven. They ran through some formalities, then Hamilton told Lauren that she wasn't under caution, though worryingly added "as yet" which depended on what information Lauren gave and any subsequent enquiries that might follow.

Lauren sat on the sofa; Geoff was beside her, Iris in an armchair. Hamilton, unlike Raven, perched on the remaining chair that somehow affirmed the less formal approach but did little to alleviate Lauren's nerves. The young officer was confident and spoke with authority, clearly a professional with ambition.

"As you're aware," Hamilton said, "Mr Leonard Thomas, your father, was seriously assaulted last night by your boyfriend Joshua Armstrong."

Lauren nodded but said nothing.

"Mr Armstrong has made a statement admitting the assault," Hamilton went on, "but we'd like you to tell us your version of what led up to the events of last night."

"I had nothing to do with what happened last night," Lauren said simply, and then added with flare: "Is Josh saying that I did?"

Hamilton made a quick note on her pad. "We have one version of events at the moment Miss Wright, so what I'm trying to establish is whether or not what you tell me corroborates with Mr Armstrong's statement."

Lauren brushed some stray hair from her eyes.

"I'd arranged to meet Josh last night over at his place," she said, guardedly. "I got a text message from him saying he was going to be a bit late. I think he said to call round at half past eight, so that's what I did. When I got to his flat he still wasn't home, and I was a bit worried. Then Gran called my mobile and told me the police wanted to talk to me. I thought Josh had had an accident or something. I've still got the texts and call history on my phone if you want to check."

Hamilton nodded but didn't seem overly interested.

"Now," Hamilton continued, "you said previously to my colleague that you thought you were being followed by your father—"

"I didn't even know I *had* a father until last night," Lauren said, her voice rising a little. "All I knew was that there was a man *looking* at me on the train home and whenever I saw him round and about he had his phone pointed at me. He even sent me some flowers! I've got photos; I can prove it." She started to scroll through the gallery images on her phone and then held the phone so the young officer could see the screen.

Hamilton gave a cursory glance but again didn't seem overly interested.

"How long do you think your dad had been following and watching you?"

Lauren thought for a moment. It was difficult to say exactly. "Maybe a month," she said quietly.

Hamilton jotted down the response in her notebook.

"Why didn't you come forward sooner?"

"I already told PC Raven why. I couldn't prove anything, except for the flowers maybe."

"We investigate the slightest concerns, Miss Wright," Hamilton said a little uppish. "Maybe your boyfriend wouldn't have found himself in such serious trouble if you hadn't have left things."

Lauren bit down on her lip and felt the heat rush to her cheeks. Being chastised in your own home by a police officer barely in her twenties was a bit humiliating even if what the woman said was true. Hamilton made some more notes and then pushed on.

"Did you feel threatened at all by your father's actions?"

"I felt uncomfortable," Lauren said truthfully. She glanced across at her grandma who was shaking her head in disbelief.

"But not threatened?" Hamilton asked.

"Maybe, I don't know."

"Did you change your travel habits in any way?"

"If I saw him at Leeds station I'd avoid him," Lauren said.

Hamilton nodded, scribbled something else.

"When you confided in your boyfriend, what was his reaction?"

"He was angry with me for not saying anything sooner."

"Did he hint or give any indication that he wanted to take matters into his own hands?"

Lauren shook her head. "He wanted me to go to the police, but I wouldn't until I had proof. I mentioned this to PC Raven yesterday."

Hamilton's radio crackled with static. Hamilton maintained a cool demeanour.

"So why do you think he did take matters into his own hands?"

"I don't know," Lauren said.

"You didn't prompt Mr Armstrong to take the action that he did?"

Before Lauren could respond, Geoff interjected: "Hang on a minute!" he said vigorously. "What kind of question's that supposed to be? Lauren hasn't done anything wrong and if you want to start suggesting otherwise we'll get a solicitor down here."

Hamilton raised a hand in supplication. "I just need to be clear that's all."

"She's already told you she had nothing to do with what's happened, that should be clear enough."

"Has Josh said something?" Lauren wanted to know.

"I don't want to say too much," Hamilton said, "but he's pretty much blaming you for what's happened."

"So he *is* saying I put him up to this?" Lauren was stunned to the core.

Hamilton pulled a face. "He says he was acting in your defence, and that you should have come to us sooner. I have to agree with the last part."

"Where's Josh now?" Lauren asked.

"He's been held on remand pending his court appearance," Hamilton said without effort. Evidently this was something she repeated a lot in her daily rounds.

"Can I visit him?"

"Perhaps in a few days' time. I'll give you some information before I leave. Technically he's not convicted, but we know he's going to enter a guilty plea. It makes a difference to the visiting rules."

Lauren sighed. She was angry with him for the trouble he'd caused yet waves of guilt dogged her. She couldn't wash her hands of things entirely.

"PC Raven said my dad's injuries were bad," Lauren said after a thought.

"They're bad enough for us not to be able to interview him yet," Hamilton said. "This was a vicious attack, Miss Wright, and it happened virtually on his own doorstep. There were quite a number of witnesses and they all more or less say the same thing."

"This is all my fault isn't it?" Lauren said, feeling ashamed. "I should have come straight to you. I'm just so stupid."

"It's complicated, Miss Wright," Hamilton said, her tone less authoritarian now. "There are two strands to this. Obviously, there's the assault, and the other is the fact that you accuse your father of stalking you. If your allegation is true, then that certainly isn't your fault. We'll check out that line of enquiry when he's able to talk to us. In the meantime we can talk to his wife."

"How the hell does a convicted rapist manage to get a wife?" Geoff said bitterly.

Hamilton shrugged. "It takes all sorts I suppose."

"So what happens now?" Lauren asked as Hamilton started to show signs of leaving.

"I'll speak with my colleagues to see where there are areas of conflict, if any, regarding what Josh has already told us, and of course, we'll need to speak to your father. I can't say for certain, but from what you've told me I think it's highly unlikely you'll need to be interviewed under caution."

Hamilton's words in this regard were welcome, coming so soon after Raven had hinted at the same thing. The officer went on: "You might still have to appear in court regardless

149

of Mr Armstrong's plea to provide them with the background information and answer any questions they might have."

Lauren nodded, wary of the prospect of officialdom and wigs.

"And what about my dad, should I visit him?"

Iris answered before the police officer could answer.

"No, Lauren!" The look of horror on her face gave no room for doubt about what she thought of that idea.

Hamilton jingled her car keys.

"I wouldn't advise it before we've spoken to him," she said. "If he admits to stalking you then you have to decide whether or not to apply for an enforcement order or not. It'll complicate matters if you're in contact with him. If he denies stalking you, then it's a choice of whether to build a case and take him to court or leave things alone. There might still be certain restrictions you can apply for even if he does deny things so don't delete any photos or messages from your phone, our IT guys might need to lift those from you."

Hamilton then handed Lauren some leaflets from her satchel, giving guidance about prison visiting rules, her rights should she be interviewed under caution and the government websites she could visit. Lauren gave them a cursory glance.

"Try not to feel so bad," Hamilton said as she made for the door. "Your boyfriend is violent and dangerous and that's why he's on remand." She smiled and looked a bit more human. "I'll wish you all a good afternoon."

31

Lauren didn't feel in the least bit reassured by what PC Hamilton had said, in fact, the only thing she could be sure of was that there were going to be stormy days ahead. Not everything had sunk in yet; she was still reeling over her dad's reappearance and Josh's internment. Her world had been blasted apart with the clumsy efficiency of an atom bomb and she unwittingly was the central player. Her gran was mooching around in the kitchen, opening and closing drawers a bit too noisily while her grandad bagged some rubbish to take to the dustbin as Lauren padded through and leaned against the open door. She waited for her gran to say something. Her mood was horribly reminiscent of the time when she'd slapped Lauren. She shot a withering look at her granddaughter and began to unload the dishwasher.

"How you can even consider seeing that man is beyond me," Iris said sorely.

"I told you, I want to know why he didn't want me or Mum."

"Because he's a piece of shit, that's why." Iris's tone was barbed and venomous. Lauren was taken aback. It was rare for her gran to swear and the look in her eyes was almost murderous. "You should throw the book at him for all the trouble he's caused."

Lauren didn't reply and watched her gran as she pulled plates and cutlery from the dishwasher, thumping them down hard on the kitchen table.

"You've got some serious thinking to do, my girl." She was full of resentment as well as anger, her hostile expression a perfect match for her choleric temper. Lauren turned away.

"I'm going to my room," she said being careful not to enflame her gran further.

When she got to her room she called Pritvia, desperate for some sympathetic counsel. She felt wracked with guilt about Josh and how awkward things were at home.

"Why should *you* feel guilty?" Pritvia said once Lauren had offloaded. "You weren't the one who started throwing your fists around. Anyway, even if you'd gone to the police sooner, the truth would still have come out about your dad."

"I know that," Lauren said with a hint of frustration. "It's just that I feel as if I don't know anyone any more. Gran and Grandad have turned out to be brilliant liars even if they meant well, and Josh is a loose cannon whom the police say is dangerous."

"He's behind bars, Lauren. They don't bang you up if you're Peppa Pig. Are you going to see him?"

"Not before he's been to court."

"I don't envy you. You're going to finish with him, right?"

"He's not going to take it very well."

"He'll have to deal with it. Imagine if he'd lost his temper with you. Violent men never change, think on that."

It was this thought that did at least assuage some of Lauren's feelings of guilt. Josh's tendency to hit out would no doubt have surfaced at some point in their relationship, and it could well be her lying in intensive care next time.

"I'm fed up with thinking," Lauren said. "I just want to turn my brain off."

32

"Why did you do it, Josh?"

They were facing each other across a simple table. The room itself was fairly basic, though relatively spacious. There was no hiding the fact that the atmosphere was oppressive, unhappy. The murmur of muted conversation dotted around the place gave a sense of something that resembled normality in this otherwise closed and abnormal world. Lauren hadn't known what to expect, her only idea of prison life were the comedies and dramas she'd seen on television. The reality was far grimmer than she was prepared for. There were too many locked doors. Her gran and grandad had wanted to come along to support her, even if that meant just waiting in the car, but Lauren had insisted she visit Josh alone. Now as she faced him, clad in his prison issue clothing, which was as grey and as sombre as a rainy day, he looked tired and drawn but otherwise healthy. Josh avoided eye contact with Lauren as he answered, preferring to keep his head bowed.

"I never intended to hit him, I just wanted to warn him off," he said. "I knew you didn't really want to go to the police so I thought if I could just have a word in his shell-like maybe that would be enough."

"So what happened?"

"When I challenged him he tried to make a run for it, so I put him to the floor. I wanted answers, but all I saw was the face that's tormented you for months. I didn't know what was in his head, all I did know was that for some reason he wanted you. I couldn't allow him to cause you any more worry, so I lost it and belted him. I couldn't stop. Every time I hit him I thought this is for Lauren… this is for Lauren… this is for Lauren…"

"No, Josh. I'd never ask you to do anything like that."

"Yeah, well if you'd have gone to the police like I wanted you to, I wouldn't be in here would I?" There was bitterness in his voice.

Lauren was all too aware of the painful truth in his words, they'd been thrown at her enough times already, but she was also very conscious of Josh's volatility and especially Zak's warning (bolstered by those of the police) that the lad was dangerous. The fact that he'd just verbally hit out at her with the petulance she'd seen whenever he didn't get his own way served only to raise her guard.

"You're right, I should have gone to the police," she said, "but you put yourself in here, not me." It was a tougher stance than she'd taken with him in the past but in here she didn't have to worry about him kicking off. "I take it you know that Leonard Thomas is my dad."

Josh nodded. "I thought it was a wind-up at first. I can't believe you didn't recognise your old man."

"Why would I? I've only got a wedding photo of him, and people can change a lot in twenty years. Besides, I was always told he was dead so how could I ever have thought he *was* my dad?"

Josh was quiet for a moment and then he said softly,

"I love you, Lauren."

"I know you do."

"You've never once said it to me, you know that?" He still wasn't looking at her, as if he was afraid of her response. "A scribbled note on a card hardly counts."

"Josh—" Lauren began, but he waved her down.

"You've never loved me like I love you," he lamented.

"I think you need to get some help, Josh." Lauren could feel the now familiar constriction in her throat as the urge to cry threatened to overwhelm her, but she'd promised herself there'd be no tears today.

"You're saying I'm a candidate for the funny farm?" He looked at her now.

"Josh, you've half killed my dad because you lost your temper."

"He was ruining your life."

"And what about Zak? Was he ruining my life too?"

"I didn't hit Zak."

"You grabbed him by the neck and threw him into the kitchen table!"

Josh said nothing. There was a strained silence. Eventually Lauren said: "Have your mum and dad been in touch?"

"They're scheduled for my next visit, but I'd rather see you."

Lauren looked away.

"You'll come again?"

Lauren bit down on her lip. She was going to have to be strong now.

"I'll write."

"Write? Lauren, I want to see you. You're all I ever think about."

"Josh, it has to be this way."

"No, it doesn't. In three years' time I'll be out. We could build a life together, start again."

"That isn't going to happen." Lauren's tears weren't supposed to happen either, but they were beginning to start. She fought to choke them back, took a breath and added, "I'm sorry, but I don't want a life with you, never knowing when you're going to kick off or get jealous. I don't need it. I want to make a fresh start of things."

"A fresh start?" Josh had raised his voice now. "What the fuck's that supposed to mean? I'm banged up in here and you're talking about making fresh starts? You can't just walk away; you owe me, Lauren!"

She got up and made to move away from the table, unsure of him and what he might do.

"I need to leave," she said, her voice trembling.

Josh rose now, pushed the table away and grabbed her arm. "No! You can't just walk out!"

"Ow! You're hurting. Get off, leave me alone!" Lauren tried to push him away, but his grip was dangerously strong.

An alarm sounded and several guards burst into the room, hauling Josh aside.

"I love you, Lauren!" he bellowed.

His words rang in her ears as a warden escorted her away.

33

A week later, PC Hamilton called to see Lauren. It was the middle of the afternoon and ordinarily she would have been at work, but she'd been granted leave on compassionate grounds and was glad of it. She was emotionally exhausted, not only due to recent events, but also because of the pressure her grandparents were applying in trying to stop her making any contact with her dad, even though they kept telling her it was her choice. This had caused numerous rows followed by periods of brooding silence, but Lauren was holding firm. She would decide what she was going to do once the police let her know the outcome of their interviews with him. It looked as if now was the time.

Lauren answered the door and showed Hamilton into the living room where her grandparents were sullenly lounging. She took the lead, offered the PC a drink, which she declined, and prepared herself for the latest developments.

"We've spoken to your father," Hamilton said, remaining on her feet despite the offer of a seat. "He hasn't exactly admitted to stalking you, but he does say he's being 'showing an interest', to use his words."

Geoff grunted. "Showing an interest? Where was his bloody interest twenty years ago?"

Lauren ignored her grandad's comment. "How did he find me?"

Hamilton shrugged. "Social media, makes everyone a private investigator these days; it won't have been difficult."

"I suppose it's a coincidence that he catches the same train home as Lauren," Iris said with contempt. "Of course he's been stalking her!"

"If you want to press charges we can look into it," Hamilton said.

"Of course we're going to press charges!" Iris said as if anything to the contrary would be ludicrous.

"Gran!" Lauren said, voice rising. "It isn't up to you."

"That man has put you through hell, Lauren." Iris wasn't budging. She then said to Hamilton, "What do we need to do to get this man out of Lauren's life?"

Hamilton looked warily at Iris, then at Lauren and it was to her she replied. "Even if you don't want to pursue a stalking charge, you'd still have to prosecute if you wanted to get a restraining order," she said. "You'd have to go to court for that."

"I want to see him," Lauren said determinedly.

"If you're intending to take matters further that might not help your case, but having said that, he is your father."

Iris got to her feet. "He's never been her father!" She looked directly at Lauren; her eyes were narrow, full of pain and frustration. Any last hope that Lauren might change her mind about meeting her dad was gone. "How can you do this? We've given you everything. Is this how you want to repay our love, by slapping us both right in our faces?"

"You'd know all about that, wouldn't you?" Lauren regretted the words as soon as she'd said them. "I'm sorry," she said, "I-I didn't mean to say that."

Hamilton did not feel at ease as the domestic threatened to boil over, and to regain some sort of control said: "These are difficult decisions and I suggest you all think about things carefully."

Iris turned away and glowered at Geoff. "Are you just going to sit there and do nothing?"

Geoff rubbed his forehead as if he were trying to iron smooth his furrowed brow. "Not now, Iris," he said. "We all need to take some breaths."

"I'm not going to change my mind," Lauren said resolutely. "He's my dad."

"I just don't know what's got into you these days my girl," Iris said, sitting on the sofa.

"What's got into me?" Lauren didn't try to hide the astonishment in her voice. "I can't believe you even have to ask."

Hamilton spoke up while she'd got the chance.

"I'm going to leave you people to sort your own heads out," she said. "You know where I am if you need any advice or guidance. I'll see myself out."

Once she'd gone, Lauren went into the hallway and pulled on a jacket, snatching her car keys from the key hook close by.

"Lauren? Where are you going?" Iris called.

The only reply was the sound of the front door being slammed closed.

Lauren drove to forty-five Sycamore Grove and parked directly in front of the driveway, staring at her dad's house for a long time. How long had he lived here without her knowing? How many times had their paths crossed without her ever realising? Other questions burned in her mind too, questions that had wheeled round her brain ever since she'd found out that her dad was alive. Why had he been watching her movements all these weeks when he might have approached her directly? Why after so long was he now 'taking an interest'? However much she tried to fathom some answers, her reasoning merely raised more questions. She couldn't say for certain if she had any intention of knocking on the door as she ruminated over things and had no idea whether her dad was still in hospital or here at home. The silver Volkswagen was in the drive, which certainly suggested someone was in. What if I knock on the door and his wife answers? she thought, trying to muster some courage to get out of the car. How much does she know about all of this? Lauren was vaguely aware of having feelings for this man she did not know. It wasn't love or affection she felt, that was for sure, but notwithstanding the man's faults, some part of him existed in her and that tie seemed binding in a way she didn't understand. She was his flesh and blood and had a right to know the answers to every question that tumbled in her brain, regardless of the wishes of her grandparents. Yes, they were both upset, desperate to keep her away from her dad, probably feeling betrayed at the moment, but that didn't matter. Everything had changed. For all that Lauren loved them both, she knew deep within herself that she'd lost some respect for them. Their well-intended lies were still lies after all and on reflection Lauren wished they'd been straight with her from the outset. So her dad wasn't perfect, he'd committed a serious crime, run out on her mother before Lauren was even born, could those truths ever really be hidden? Surely her grandparents must have known there was a chance that her dad might show up again at some point even though they'd claimed they never thought it a possibility. Or maybe they'd just buried their heads in the sand. Whatever they'd hoped to achieve was now irrelevant as fate had delivered its unerring hand leaving Lauren to deal with the assault on her emotions. She closed her eyes, felt the quick, rhythmic thumping of her heart, the dryness in her throat, her body trembling. She knew she couldn't bottle things up any longer. It was time to get some answers before she went mad. She reached into her bag for her notebook, tore out a page and scribbled a message suggesting that she and her dad should meet at a safe, neutral venue. The only place she could think of was the Ridings shopping arcade in Wakefield. It would be busy with shoppers but there was a decent coffee bar there. It might not be intimate or private, but she needed to feel safe and surrounded by people. She read through her note several times before she decided it was okay. Her handwriting wasn't at its best given the state of her nerves, but it was legible. She got out of her car and walked down the driveway. Once she got to the front door, she took several breaths before slipping the note through the letterbox. There was no going back now.

34

L auren wasn't looking forward to going home because she had no intention of lying to her grandparents about where she'd been. She was rapidly coming to the conclusion that after everything that had happened, living at home was likely to become untenable. She'd said to Josh that she wanted to make a fresh start and knowing that life with her grandparents was almost certainly going to be strained from now on, her first embryonic thoughts of flying the nest started to seriously ruminate in her mind.

Once she got home she saw that her grandad's BMW was missing from the driveway. She'd forgotten he was working afternoon shifts this week and he wouldn't be home until half past ten. It meant that she couldn't get things over with in one go if things kicked off.

Her gran was in the kitchen rolling out some pastry when she came in.

"Nice of you let me know what time you'd be home," Iris said pressing down hard on the roller.

"I'm not late am I?" Lauren said, guardedly.

"I wouldn't know; you don't say where you're going these days and slammed doors have a certain finality to them." She hadn't looked at Lauren since she came in and continued to roll out the pastry.

"I went down to Dad's," Lauren said, sounding far more confident than she felt. The rolling pin still worked hard, but for the briefest of instants Lauren detected a slight pause in its movement. She waited for a response and got none. "I pushed a note through the letterbox asking him to get in touch."

Iris looked darkly at her granddaughter.

"You did what?"

"It was just my email address, nothing else."

"So you really are determined to betray your grandad and me." Her tone was as hard as frozen metal.

"I'm not betraying you," Lauren said, clearly hurt by the suggestion. "Can't you try to see things from my point of view for once?"

"How can *you* have a point of view?" Iris spat. "If you could only have seen the hurt that man caused your mother, is still causing us all, you wouldn't give him a second of your day."

Lauren had heard most of this argument before over the past few days and the last thing she wanted was to rake over old ground. It was clear they would never agree.

"I have to find that truth for myself," Lauren said.

"God help you when I tell your grandad about this," Iris said bitterly.

"I'm fed up with arguing," Lauren said. "I know you don't like it, but it's my life and you don't have the right to stop me seeing my own dad."

"I never knew you could be so cruel," Iris said. "You were brought up to have respect and manners. You're a different person these days."

Lauren flinched at her gran's words. "Everything I once believed in has gone," she said, raising her voice now. "Am I supposed to just take it?"

"What you're supposed to do, my girl, is have some gratitude for what your grandad and me have done for you over the years. Obviously our efforts mean nothing to you."

"That's not true," Lauren protested.

Iris started rolling the pastry again. She looked to be on the verge of tears. "We've done everything to protect you from that man," she sniffed. "We're the ones who brought you up, clothed and fed you, saw you had a good education and gave you all our love and emotional support while he was playing around and raping women. I can't understand you at all."

Lauren couldn't see any way through the impasse.

"My wanting to see Dad has got nothing to do with what you and Grandad have done for me. There's so much about Dad that I just don't know about."

"You know all there is to know."

"I didn't know he was alive; I think that was pretty important."

Iris took a breath, drawing on her last reserves of patience. "Is this how it's going to be from now on, Lauren, throwing things back in our faces?"

"I didn't ask for any of this to happen," Lauren countered, trying to keep on an even keel.

Iris blinked through her tears as she worked the pastry, but she didn't say anything. Lauren turned away.

"I'm going to my room," she said, moodily.

Iris watched as Lauren went through into the living room. When she heard her run up the stairs, she held her hands over her face and choked back her tears.

35

L auren played with her phone for over an hour as she lay back on her bed, distracting herself from the shit in her life. She wished she had friends a little closer to home and regretted not keeping in touch with those she once had, but since she'd established a new working life, many had dropped away like autumn leaves. Most of those who'd been at her party had now moved on to pastures new in one way or another and remaining friends on the various social platforms didn't really count. What she needed was somewhere to crash for a few days. She didn't want to impose herself on Pritvia and her family, and the only other person she could think of was Zak, he at least had his own place, but he was miles away in London.

Maybe that's where I need to be, away from everything, she thought as she brought up Zak's Facebook profile. It didn't look like Zak had been uploading much lately, perhaps he was too busy. As she'd already visited him on several occasions for long weekends, maybe she could arrange to go down and stay for a bit longer once she'd seen her dad and copped for the inevitable fallout at home. She looked at the time. It was half past five. He wouldn't be home for another hour so she sent a text saying she would call him at seven. She'd regularly kept him in the loop over what was going on, he'd understand how awkward her home life was becoming, there was a chance he might invite her down. The prospect of staying with Zak lifted her spirits somewhat, but she cautioned herself not to be presumptuous. He had a life of his own to lead and she might not fit in. Feeling hungry, she went downstairs. Her gran was watching news on the television. Something smelled good in the oven and Lauren said so.

"It's meat and potato pie. It'll be ready in twenty minutes," Iris said.

Lauren might have been hungry, but she really wasn't overly enamoured with the idea of carbs and fattening pastry. Still, she'd suffer it rather than cause more conflict.

"I'll set the table," she said.

"You don't have to."

"I usually do."

"Suit yourself."

Lauren allowed her gran's barbed replies to wash over her, though their sting was pushing her patience to its limits. The countless times she'd helped her gran with the pre-meal kitchen duties was usually a light-hearted affair, but the cold wall of silence that now prevailed was torturous. In an effort to keep her mind off the charged atmosphere, Lauren took the initiative in serving the meal, forcing her gran to the dining table. Lauren's discomfort as they both ate was driving her to despair, her gran making no attempt to instigate any kind of a thaw.

Finally Lauren had had enough and pushing her plate aside said, "I can't stand any more of this. You're making me feel like I'm something a dog's thrown up. I'm sick of it."

"You can always go to your room."

Lauren was seething at her gran's stony attitude, but she remained controlled. "I know how Josh felt now. You're not so different from his mum and dad; no wonder he couldn't wait to move out."

"And a fine mess he's made of things."

Lauren ignored the remark. "I wish I'd got my own place," she said. "It's too toxic round here."

"You know the reason for that."

"What are you frightened of?"

"I'm not frightened of anything."

"Yes you are, Gran, both you and Grandad. Do you think I'm going to play you and Dad off one another, is that it?"

"You're being ridiculous."

"I'm not," Lauren said indignantly.

"Go to your room Lauren," Iris said, dangerously close to breaking point. "I don't want to talk about this until your grandad gets home."

"He won't be home for ages yet," Lauren said. "And I'm not talking about this any more." She got up. "You should know I'm thinking of going down to Zak's for a while. It's either that or go mad in this place."

Iris saw the resolute look on Lauren's face as she withdrew and knew that the granddaughter she once had was no longer the girl she had been. She wouldn't dare slap her across the face now.

Offloading to Zak was cathartic, especially when you had one eye on his place as a bolthole away from madness. He'd listened with sympathy, made all the right noises in all the right places which encouraged Lauren's confidence in asking if she could come down to stay for a few days.

"Are you sure it won't make things worse at home for you?" he asked after agreeing to her request.

"I don't think they could be much worse," Lauren said pragmatically. "Besides, I need space to think. I might have to get away altogether."

"Sounds like your world's changing fast."

"I feel like I'm only just hanging onto the railings. I hardly know myself these days. I don't even know what I actually want from my dad. I've got lots of questions, but he's a total stranger and I haven't decided if I even want him in my life. He's caused enough trouble as it is."

"Yeah," Zak agreed. "He hasn't half. I take it you're cutting ties completely with Josh?"

"I said I'd write to him."

"And will you?"

"Yes."

"Make sure he understands there's no going back."

"I will."

"So when do you want to come down?"

"I'll phone on Sunday. I'll need to arrange to take time off work."

"Cool."

Geoff got home just before eleven p.m. Lauren had long since retired to bed but as was usual lately, she wasn't really sleeping. She could hear her gran telling him all about her day and in particular Lauren's visit to her dad's. She made a meal of their subsequent stand-off afterwards. Her gran described Lauren as intransigent and wilful, her attitude being deliberately provocative. Lauren was annoyed as well as bemused as she strained to hear her grandparents and was tempted to confront them, but she reasoned that would only confirm what her gran was saying so she deferred for the moment. Worryingly, she heard her grandad say that he would have 'words with her in the morning'. She hunkered down between the sheets, but it was a mild night and there was no comfort there. Perhaps it would be better to haul herself out of bed and get things over with now as late as it was. It wasn't as if she needed to be up for work in the morning. Deciding this was the best course of action to take, she pulled on her nightie and padded downstairs, adrenaline gushing through her veins in anticipation of the confrontation she was certain would come. When she walked into the living room, her grandparents were sitting together on the sofa looking preoccupied.

"I heard you talking about me," Lauren said, keeping her tone as plain and matter-of-fact as she could.

Her grandparents exchanged looks.

"You're giving us plenty to talk about," Geoff said, putting down the mug of hot chocolate he'd been drinking onto a side table.

"I'm fed up with all of this," Lauren said. "I've done nothing wrong."

"It's late, I think this should wait until morning."

Lauren could feel the warm prickle of tears begin to well up in her eyes. She was exhausted with the strain of everything and the one place she was desperate for support was in her own home.

"I don't want this," she said, her voice beginning to tremble. "I hate everything that's happened." She sat in an armchair, wrestling with her emotions.

"None of us want this," Geoff said, plainly.

"Why are you making it seem that everything's my fault?" Lauren sniffed.

Geoff sighed. "I must have said this a hundred times Lauren, it's not that we think things are your fault; we don't want you to get involved with your dad."

"I just want to talk to him."

"It won't end there, Lauren."

"Why are you so scared of me seeing him?"

Geoff massaged his temples and closed his eyes as if encumbered by the world.

"I'll have to tell her, Iris," he said. "She's going to find out anyway."

Lauren's heart missed several beats, and she bit down on her lip, her large eyes staring expectantly at her grandad as she waited with anticipation for yet another revelation.

"Oh, Geoff," Iris said, on the verge of tears herself now.

Lauren could plainly see her grandad's uneasiness; the awkward and pained look on his face, as if everything hung on what he was about to say.

"The fact of things, Lauren," he started falteringly, "is that we paid your dad to keep away from you. It was a substantial amount, and he took it. We thought it might make him stay dead once he was released from prison, obviously he's had a change of mind."

"God, this gets worse," Lauren said as the tears trickled down her cheeks. "How much was I worth for him to keep away?"

"It's not about your worth, Lauren," Iris said, her heart breaking. "We love you more than anything in the world; you *are* our world."

"How much did you pay him?" Lauren asked again.

"Twenty thousand," Geoff said. "We paid him twenty thousand."

Lauren was numbed into silence.

So that's what I'm worth to him, she thought. *And it's what they think I'm worth too. Twenty thousand pounds!*

"Well, now I know my price," she said, even more upset now.

"It was everything we could afford to keep him from you," Iris said, though her words sounded limp.

"I feel sick," Lauren said.

Geoff got up from the sofa. "I'm sorry about everything, Lauren," he said. "We thought we were doing our best for you. We don't like the idea of your dad being involved in your life, but we can't stop you if you want to see him. It's just that it feels like your gran and me are being pushed aside for a man you don't even know, a man who's caused a lot of trouble for us all."

Lauren sat in silence, hardly able to believe what she'd just heard. Her grandparents had hardly played a blinder with their so-called good intentions, yet the fact that her dad had been bought off by them was even worse. Twenty grand had been more important to him than getting to know his own daughter. As far as her grandparents were concerned, she was plainly mystified. She was well aware of everything they had done for her; without question they loved her and had supported her in every way they could, even if the large gap in their respective generations clashed at times. She'd never had to pay for a driving lesson; they'd bought her a car for her eighteenth birthday; they'd been generous with her allowance before she'd found a job, treated her to clothes, shows, trips away, in fact the whole icing. These were the fruits of a love that was unequivocal, yet they had hurt her on a level she didn't know was possible, and certainly not one she could define. She could feel anger and frustration battling for supremacy, pulling her mind from side to side like some psychic game of tug-of-war, and even though these feelings weren't strangers to her, they were becoming a bit too familiar these days. In her final analysis, she couldn't help feeling like she was some sort of commodity. She got up from the chair.

"Where are you going?" Iris asked apprehensively.

"To bed," Lauren said. "Where else would I be going?"

They left her to it. When Lauren climbed back into bed she was as wide awake as the midday sun. Eventually she did sleep, but not before she'd replayed everything she'd just learned over and over in her mind. When she awoke, she saw that it had gone ten, which was late for her even when she wasn't at work. What sleep she'd managed had not refreshed her though. Her head ached and she felt spaced out. She needed Saturday to come fast because today was going to be awkward.

Her grandparents were already up. Geoff was watching the news as Lauren sauntered uneasily into the living room. She could hear Iris unloading the dishwasher in the kitchen and managed to utter a weak "Good morning" to her grandad.

"Good morning, love," Geoff said. It was pointless asking how she was feeling, her blanched and tired complexion told him all he needed to know. "What are your plans today?" It was a good question.

"I don't know, maybe I'll go into town."

"No friends you can spend time with?"

"They're all at work."

Geoff reached into his pocket and pulled out his wallet. He fished out a wad of notes and handed them over to Lauren.

"What's this for?" she said.

"Treat yourself to something. A dress, new shoes, a bag."

Lauren pushed the money aside. "You've bought me once already."

177

Geoff took the remark on the chin. "It's a peace offering," he said.

"I don't want it."

"So what can your gran and me do to make things right?"

"I don't know."

Iris came through. "Do you want something to eat?"

"I'll get my own, thank you."

"I'm making an omelette for your grandad. It's no trouble."

"I'm going into town; I'll get something there."

"What time will you be home?"

"I don't know."

Iris sighed. It wasn't so long since Lauren would map out her day and tell them both exactly what she'd be doing, where'd she'd be going and what time she'd be home. Any variation to her plans would undoubtedly bring a phone or text message. How things had changed.

"Some idea would be nice."

"Gran, I can hardly think at the moment. Stop pestering me."

Iris was about to bite back but Geoff raised a hand.

"All right, all right," he said. "Let's not get into any arguments today." He faced Lauren. "Do as you do, love, just don't get us worrying any more than we are already."

"I won't," she said without warmth, and went through into the kitchen. Her grandparents could hear the kettle click on.

"Do you think she'll ever forgive us?" Iris asked, not really wanting an answer.

36

Lauren spent a couple of hours in town. She called into Shakespeare's Café where her dad had sat so close to her only a few weeks ago and ordered a latté and scrambled egg on toast. As she tried to relax, her phoned beeped signalling that she had an email. Her heart skipped several beats as she saw that it was in response to the note she'd given her dad the other day. The email wasn't from her dad, however, but his wife. It read:

Lauren,

I passed your note over to your father. He isn't due out of hospital until the middle of next week. He is of course keen to meet you. Either he or I will confirm a day and a time once he is back at home. We both think that it is a good idea to meet somewhere public.

Regards,

Kate

She read the email through several times and exhaled some calming breaths. The response had arrived quicker than she'd thought it might, which was good. It meant that both sides wanted to bring things to a head, one way or another.

At half past one she headed off home but detoured to forty-five Sycamore Grove on the way back. She was here through compulsion, as if being in the very presence of the house could give her some clarity of mind. This was the house of answers, the house that held her future in its hands. She imagined what she might say to her dad when she finally did meet him, and endlessly ran scenarios through her brain, never once taking her eyes off the house. Perhaps this time next week she'd be a whole lot wiser.

When she got home she was relieved to see that her grandparents were out. Her grandad was at work again, but she'd no idea where her gran was. Perhaps she was visiting some friends. In contradiction to her own idealism, Iris hadn't seen fit to let Lauren know where she was going. The time alone gave Lauren the chance to put pen to paper and write to Josh as she'd promised. After several false starts she managed to compose something that she thought was satisfactory, sealed the envelope and put the letter to one side. It wasn't time to post it yet.

It was mid-Thursday afternoon when Lauren received another email.

Lauren,

Your father would like to meet this coming Saturday if that is convenient. The Toscana coffee bar in the Ridings shopping centre would be good. Is two p.m. okay with you?

Regards,

Kate

Lauren's return email confirmed that it was. Now the clock really was ticking.

When Saturday arrived, Lauren had never felt so nervous in all her life. Iris and Geoff weren't at their best either. Lauren, making a rare first move these days, told them she was setting off early, she couldn't hang around the house until it was time to meet her dad. It didn't surprise Lauren that her gran was visibly upset, though to see her grandad on the verge of tears certainly was surprising. As Lauren grabbed her car keys, Iris dashed over and hugged her. It was an embrace of yearning and pain, and Lauren was in no way insensitive to it.

"I love you so much," Iris agonised, "there just aren't the words…"

"It's all right," Lauren said tightly, not entirely sure what she actually meant.

Iris pulled back, appraised her granddaughter. "You look lovely," she said.

Lauren had made the effort that was for sure. She was quite formally dressed in a checked jacket, a white blouse and dark trousers. She didn't look quite the little girl any more. Perhaps that was her intention.

Lauren managed a smile. "Thank you."

"I really wish you weren't going."

"I know."

"You'll always be our little girl, Lauren, never forget that."

They watched as Lauren got into her car and then drive quickly up the road. She didn't wave or give a friendly blast of the horn as was her usual habit. Her expression had been one of grim determination.

"Things are never going to be the same, Iris," Geoff said as Lauren turned the corner. "We're just going to have to hang on in there."

"I'm not sure if I can," Iris said inconsolably.

37

Time passed slowly but the throng of the Ridings kept Lauren sane. There were times when she almost forgot that she was meeting her dad as she browsed the shops which she supposed was a good thing, but her stomach did somersaults when her mind eventually dragged her thoughts back his way. At a quarter to two, she nipped to the toilet before she made her way over to the coffee bar, which was at the far end of the arcade. She ordered herself a latté. It was always good coffee here, but today it tasted vile in her parched mouth. As two thirty approached, Lauren's nerves were hanging by their threads. Her heart hardly knew whether to beat faster or stop altogether. She cast her eyes around the heaving crowds searching for any sign of her dad. *What if he doesn't show up,* she thought as she messed with her phone, staring blankly at Instagram that ordinarily would at least hold some interest for her. She worked some saliva into her mouth and licked her dry lips. *Is he going to bail at the last minute*, she wondered? *I'm not sure I can stand much more of this.* She checked the time and was convinced that the hands on her watch were going backwards. Ten minutes. Ten minutes was a lifetime. Perhaps this is what it felt like on Death Row just before your time to fry. She tried to distract herself by checking her hair and make-up, but nothing was going to calm her cannoning heart. She could feel her stomach burn and her acids rise, and for a moment she thought she might throw up, but a sip of coffee seemed to steady her insides as noxious as it was. She looked at her watch again: barely a minute had passed. She closed her eyes and tried to soothe the butterflies in her gut, but the more she tried the worse it got. To add to her discomfort, she was desperate for the toilet again. If she was quick, she might just manage it before her dad showed. As she got up from her seat, she glanced to her left towards the main entryway back into the arcade and saw him weaving his way through the throng. She immediately sat back down and could feel herself shaking; her mind was as blank as death. She could see him searching for her and unbelievably she found herself waving across at him. He acknowledged and came across. Lauren could see that he looked nervous. His pale and drawn cheeks, yellowed and stained with deep bruising made him appear a shadow of his former self. Lauren saw that he'd made the effort to look trim, dressed in a tweed jacket and dark trousers. She stood as he came to the table and regarded him apprehensively. It was clear to her that her dad felt as awkward as she did and he'd no real idea of how to greet her. In the end he nodded self-consciously and asked her if she wanted a drink.

"I'll have a latté please," Lauren said quietly; her barren throat was desperately in need of quenching. The second coffee couldn't be as bad as the first. Her dad turned and went over to the counter. Lauren sat back down and tried to compose herself, hardly able to believe that this moment had actually arrived. Presently her dad returned with their drinks. Lauren immediately sipped her latté. It still tasted vile.

They sat uncomfortably for what seemed a year before Lauren bravely said, "Aren't you going to say something?"

Her dad nodded and cast his watery eyes into hers. "I suppose I'd better start by asking how you are."

"Nervous," Lauren said.

"Same here," her dad replied. There was another silence. He looked into his drink as if somehow magical words might appear and tell him what to say next. "Thanks for this," he said, showing Lauren the note she'd pushed through his door. "I know it can't have been easy, especially after everything that's happened, I'd no idea that I scared you or that you even knew I was following you."

"I had nothing to do with what Josh did," Lauren said.

Her dad waved a dismissive hand. "I probably deserved a good kicking. Maybe I've had it coming for years."

"Your face is a bit of a mess."

"It looks worse than it feels."

The introductory exchange was filled with nervous tension and as a result they fell into several minutes of trivial conversation while they settled themselves down. Eventually Lauren, who seemed to settle the quickest, took the initiative in pushing things forward.

"I thought you were dead," she said.

Her dad gave a short scoffing laugh. "That's what they told you is it?"

"Among other things."

"I should imagine your gran and grandad have said quite a lot."

Lauren shrugged and got straight to the point.

"They told me they paid you twenty thousand pounds to stay out of my life, so why haven't you?" She made no attempt to hide the bitterness in her voice.

Her dad was staring down into the depths of his coffee, swirling it around in his hand.

"Shortly before I was due for release your grandparents got in touch and made me the offer. I'd got absolutely nothing, no job, no home to call my own, I needed to survive, get back on my feet, so I agreed. I reasoned that as I'd never known you I might as well take the money."

"Did you think you got a good price for me?"

He shook his head.

"It was survival."

Lauren thought about his answer for a few moments.

"Was it a hard decision, taking the money?"

She could see a vein pulsing on her dad's forehead as he weighed the question.

"I didn't know you," he said without meeting her eye. "I've done some bad things, Lauren. I'm not going to hide away from that, but a bloke can start again can't he? Make amends for what he got wrong?"

"How can you make amends?" Lauren said. "You can't un-rape that woman or turn back the clock and be the dad I wanted."

Lauren's dad looked ashamed. "When I was in the slammer and up for parole, I saw a counsellor. She helped me a lot, cleared my head of all the shit that had been in my brain. It was a long job and she helped me through it all. In the end our relationship became less professional, and we hooked up together."

"Kate?"

"Kate, yes. She saved me in more ways than one."

Lauren wasn't sure what he meant by this exactly, but she didn't challenge the statement. Instead, she offloaded the one question that had burned inside her like molten lead ever since she'd learned of her dad's existence.

"Why didn't you want to be with me or Mum?"

His face flushed. "Because I wasn't ready for either of you. I was a coward and so I shot through. I hid my head in the sand and got involved with the wrong sorts, did drugs and went totally off the rails. I was a bloody fool. But my head's straight now, I'm not who or what I was… I started thinking about you, what you might be doing and getting up to. I wanted to see you, get to know you."

"You could have written."

He shook his head. "When I took the money I agreed I wouldn't make contact; besides, from what you've said how would a letter from the grave have gone down?"

Lauren had to concede that point. "But you've been following me."

188

"Yes."

"For how long?"

"Six months, maybe a bit more."

Lauren's jaw dropped wide open. "Six months!"

Her dad nodded. "Ever since Kate and me moved up here to be exact."

"You moved to be near me?"

"Partly. Kate needed to relocate up north for her work and I said I wanted to be close to you. She took quite a bit of persuading on that part I can tell you."

"Because she knew you'd follow me?"

He shook his head.

"She knew all about the arrangement I had with Geoff and Iris. In the end I assured her I wouldn't try to contact you, I just wanted to see my own daughter in the flesh." A melancholy expression crossed his face and he stared into his coffee. "I hoped to catch sight of you by walking past your house at certain times over a weekend. Sometimes I'd get lucky, and I'd see you as you were getting into your car or taking some rubbish to the bin, that sort of thing, but it was a poor return really. Not that I deserved more, though I couldn't believe my luck when I saw that we both caught the same train home. From that moment I made a point of watching out for you at the station. I kept my distance, snapped some photos and videos if I could, but the more I saw of you, the closer I wanted to get. The photos only made me want you more. Believe it or not, I felt a kind of love for you, and that's probably when you started to notice me."

"How could you love me?"

189

Her dad shifted in his seat and sipped his drink.

"Can you ever explain love?"

"Gran and Grandad love me. You don't even know me. Did you ever love Mum?"

"You ask very difficult questions, Lauren."

Before he could say anything further, a mother with a pram barged past, forcing him to move his chair out of the way. When he'd settled again he said, "I thought I loved your mum. I wouldn't have married her otherwise."

"Were you seeing other women while you were married to her?"

Her dad's discomfort looked worse than his bruising did. "Lauren, I'd like to talk about *us*."

"You can't blame me for asking questions," Lauren said a little defensively. "What did you expect?"

Her dad shrugged his shoulders and sipped his coffee.

"I'm not proud of my past Lauren."

She studied him as he fell silent. *He's so weak,* she thought. He certainly didn't look like a man who had once been so reckless and malfeasant in his youth. He looked older than her grandad as he sat hunched over his coffee.

"I didn't expect an easy ride," he said at length. "I just hoped…" As his voice tailed off it was apparent that another uncomfortable silence would follow which was more than Lauren could stand.

"And what about the flowers?" she asked, "What were they all about?"

Lauren's dad flushed again despite his bruising. "I wanted to give you something to cheer you up, brighten your day that's all. They weren't meant to frighten you. It was silly really, I wasn't thinking straight; you were filling my thoughts by the hour, and I just had to do something, or I'd tear myself apart. You know, the best thing that's happened to me lately is the kicking I got from your boyfriend. If he hadn't given me a pasting then we wouldn't be here today."

"You've caused a lot of trouble," Lauren said. "Gran and Grandad are terrified that I'll try to make things right with you."

"They've never liked me, even before I gave them a reason not to." He sounded resentful.

"We've argued a lot over you."

"I don't want to come between you and your grandparents. I mean… Jesus, they've raised you better than I ever could have done."

Lauren smiled thinly and felt some warmth rush to her cheeks. This show of geniality, as fleeting as it was, lifted her dad's spirits and spurred him to push further.

"Is there a chance that you and I could… that we could… build something new, get to know each other?"

Lauren bit down on her lip as her heart livened again. "Josh is in prison because of you," she said, "and it would cause too much trouble at home. A few weeks ago I didn't even know you were alive; it's all so sudden, I can hardly think."

"But there's a chance for me, surely?" There was urgency in his voice, as if the hope that was rising in him might evaporate if he didn't force things.

Lauren didn't give an answer because she didn't know how best to respond. Instead she looked at the crowds in the arcade, most folk were lumbered with heavy shopping or saddled with whining kids, or both. She would have swapped places with any of them at the moment.

"I mean, I must have a chance otherwise you wouldn't be here, right?" her dad continued. "Why else would you have pushed the note through the letterbox?"

"Because I wanted answers," Lauren said, facing him now.

"I've given you answers haven't I?"

"Yes," Lauren said fingering her mug of coffee sombrely. "and I wish none of this had happened. You should have just kept away." She could see that her words hurt him.

"I'm not the man I was, you have to believe that."

"I don't have to believe anything," Lauren countered. "You're a stranger who just happens to be my dad."

"All I'm asking for is a chance." Desperation was creeping into his voice. "I've worked damned hard to get to where I am now. I know I can be something good in your life."

"Gran and Grandad have done everything for me," Lauren said, feeling her eyes begin to well with tears. "They made a lot of sacrifices."

"And they told you lies."

"Yes," Lauren said, "and I hate that they did, but they thought they were being kind."

"Kind? They told you I was dead."

"You might as well have been. When they offered you all that money you could have turned it down, but you didn't."

"I told you; I had nothing."

"You had Kate."

"And what do you think would have happened if I had turned it down? You'd have all of this shit to deal with when you were about seven or eight years old."

"You took the money because you wanted it more than you wanted me."

"Yesterday's man took the money, Lauren."

Lauren was fighting to stay in control of her emotions as well as her nerves. "You haven't wanted anything to do with me for twenty years," she said, grabbing a tissue from her bag and blowing her nose. "Why would I want anything to do with you now?"

"I'm your dad. That must count for something, surely."

A baby started crying somewhere in the background which distracted Lauren's train of thought. It took several minutes for the baby to settle, which allowed Lauren time to gather her composure.

"I don't need you in my life," she said, her heart thumping heavily. "All you've done is cause trouble."

Her dad shifted his gaze and stared into his almost empty coffee cup. "Have you ever wanted something so badly that you physically ached? It's like having a volcano inside you ready to burst, only there's nowhere for the lava to go. You have to keep the lid on it because you know if you let what's inside spill out it'll kill you, and if you don't it might kill you anyway. You've never felt that?"

Lauren shook her head.

"You're lucky. It's what I've been living with ever since I first saw you, only it's getting worse. I can't stand much more of it."

Lauren was shocked by the rawness of the disclosure. Before she could respond her dad said: "You can take the pain away, if you'll just let me in."

Lauren bit on her lip as her eyes moistened once more.

"It's too late," she said.

"Why is it too late?"

"It just is," Lauren said. She stood up. "I think I should go home. Gran and Grandad were right, I should have just left things."

"No, Lauren, please!" He grabbed her wrist and held her firmly. "Please, Lauren, I'm begging you."

"Get off me," Lauren said, her voice trembling. She remembered Josh having done the same thing when she'd tried to leave him during her prison visit.

Her dad immediately released his grip.

"I'm sorry," he said. "I didn't mean to do that. Lauren, I'd never hurt you. I just... I just... for God's sake can't a man ever wipe a slate clean? Have I got to be punished for the rest of my life for making stupid mistakes?"

"Punished? You've got Kate, a job, friends most probably; how are you being punished?"

"You're punishing me, Lauren. I just want you to be a part of my life. You can't change the fact that I'm your dad. I'll always be that."

"I came today to get answers, nothing more." She slung her bag over her shoulder and moved away from the table. "Let me past please, I want to go home."

"You can't leave like this," her dad said without giving ground.

"You left Mum and me twenty years ago," Lauren said coolly. "We all managed fine without you, and we will again, now please let me past."

Her dad sat down and held his head in his hands. "I've tried my best, Lauren, I really have. What's the point in getting your head and life right if the mud sticks?"

"I haven't thrown any mud at you," Lauren said. "You're trying to say that I owe you something because you're my dad. I don't owe you anything."

"I didn't reckon on you being so hard."

"Hard?" Lauren steadied herself as her throat tightened. "If I was hard I'd be prosecuting you."

He recognised that he was on thin ice, but he persisted one last time.

"There's no chance for us then?"

"None," Lauren said, breaking past him.

"Lauren!"

It was no use. She was dashing down the main aisle as far from him as she could get. To his bitter disappointment, she didn't look back.

38

"I'm so relieved," Iris said as they all sat at the kitchen table with mugs of hot coffee. The strain she'd been carrying over the last few weeks had been instantly lifted. "You've done the right thing." She was tearful as she spoke, and Geoff handed her a tissue.

"I know I put you through it," Lauren said, still a bit tearful herself, "but it was something I had to get out of my system so I could draw a line. I really tried to make you understand."

"You're very brave," Geoff said. "We could have done things a bit differently, I admit, but we're proud of you, Lauren, we always have been."

Lauren blushed and smiled thinly. "There is something I need to tell you both though," she added soberly.

Geoff and Iris exchanged glances.

"Oh?" Geoff said.

"It's something I mentioned to Gran the other day. I'm going to stay with Zak in London for a few days. I need to get away for a while and be surrounded by new things and let my brain relax."

"Zak's a good lad," Geoff said.

Lauren looked a little uncomfortable. "I might want to stay down there," she added tentatively.

More exchanged glances.

"Lauren, you've been through a lot, we all have," Geoff said. "Now's not the time to make hasty decisions."

"I'm not being hasty," Lauren said. "I'm just saying what I might do."

"You've thought about it, evidently," Iris said.

"I've thought about lots of things. Anyway, I haven't even told Zak that I might want to stay down there."

"You'd stay with him?" Geoff asked.

"If he'd let me, until I found a place of my own."

"But what about your job? You love working at the university," Iris said.

"I haven't said what I will do, just what I might do."

"London's very expensive," Iris cautioned. "You could never afford to buy or rent anything decent down there working in a library."

"Gran let me just go down there and turn my brain off, please."

"Leave her alone, Iris," Geoff said calmly. "She's been through enough."

Iris reluctantly backed down, though by her expression it was clear she wasn't happy. Only minutes ago she'd been ecstatic that Lauren was distancing herself from her dad, and now she was saying she wanted distance from them too.

"It'll be all right," Lauren said, reaching across the table and taking her gran's hands in hers. Iris didn't look convinced.

Zak's apartment was everything Josh's wasn't. It was modern, spacious, fitted out with all the latest gadgets and had a view of the city to die for. Zak's wage at the private gallery where he worked certainly didn't cover the rent, but his affluent family were more than happy to fill the gap. There were distinct opportunities in London that didn't exist in little old Pontefract or in its neighbouring towns and cities and when Zak had first intimated he wished to move to London, they collectively saw it as advantageous for him to be permanently housed there. Lauren always enjoyed staying with Zak and loved the vibrancy of London life. It was a different world in The Smoke, exciting, prosperous, alluring and Lauren was sorely tempted by what it had to offer each time she visited. Once she'd dumped her bags and freshened up after the journey down, Zak took her out for a pizza at the local Italian, and over a bottle of red wine, Lauren brought him completely up to speed with everything.

"What a summer you've had," Zak said when she'd finished. "Talk about everything happening at once."

Lauren was feeling a little giddy after her third glass of wine. The alcohol hitting her brain was gradually dulling the pain of recent days. She giggled.

"I'll wake up tomorrow and it'll all have been a bad dream."

"Well at least it's all over, one way or another," Zak said, raising his glass. "Let's drink to new beginnings."

"New beginnings," Lauren echoed and drained her glass. She was smiling sheepishly at Zak now. "Do you mind if I ask you something?"

"Go on."

"Do you think I could stay and look for work down here? I mean, I'd pay my way until I found something, I have savings."

Zak was taken aback. "Well, of course it's fine with me, I could do with the company. Do you think your gran and grandad will be okay with it though?"

Lauren poured herself another glass. "I pre-warned them that it was something I was thinking about. I'm sorry if I was being presumptuous."

Zak shrugged. "You knew I'd say yes."

Lauren flushed bright red and smiled. Zak poured the last of the wine into his glass. "I can ask about at my place if you like. Sometimes jobs come up out of the blue. It'll be a start at least."

"Thank you."

"Are you sure you want to leave everything behind? You've got a good job already, you've got family, friends. Down here there's only me."

"I'd like to give it a go." Her eyes twinkled as she spoke. Zak wasn't certain whether there was a double meaning in her words.

"Well, as soon as you've sorted things your end, we'll take things a step at a time."

"I'll drink to that," Lauren said brightly. "Shall we get another bottle?"

When Lauren returned home a week later she was much more like the granddaughter that Iris and Geoff knew and loved so much. The break had clearly done her good. However, they were hardly ecstatic when she told them she intended to move in with Zak within the next few weeks, but as unpalatable as that idea was to them, anything was better than the girl being involved with her dad. Lauren promised faithfully that she'd phone them every day and come to visit them at least once a month. She seemed excited and happy again and finally, that was all that mattered.

On Monday Lauren handed in her notice much to her colleagues' disappointment. Pritvia especially was upset by the news even though she was sympathetic to Lauren's cause.

"How am I going to look after you all the way down in London?" she'd said. Lauren had passed things off as lightly as she could as well as filling her friend in on all the details of her meeting with her dad. Pritvia had questioned her with the ruthlessness of a barrister; to such an extent that Lauren thought that the girl had missed her vocation. But she loved her for it all the same. It was a strange day though, the feeling that very soon you'd be sailing on new waters was as scary as it was exciting, but the once secure and safe world that Lauren had known for years had proved to be an impostor and it had changed her markedly. All day at work her thoughts had been of London, Zak and new horizons. Her buoyant mood was soon torpedoed however as she arrived at the station hoping to catch the 17.22 to

Fitzwilliam. There was major rail disruption running between Leeds and Doncaster that directly affected her journey. No one knew how long any delays would last and several trains had been cancelled already. Lauren felt waves of frustration wash through her as she searched her phone for updates, but she knew she'd have to make for Pontefract, the faithful old bolthole when things went wrong on the Doncaster line. She called her gran, doing her best to hide her irritation at the chaotic situation and arranged for her customary lift, all the time keeping a look out for her dad. Thankfully, he wasn't anywhere around. She reasoned that he was either keeping his distance or catching another train. In a few days' time it would hardly matter anyway. Forty minutes later, Lauren arrived at Pontefract; her gran was dutifully waiting for her in her Mini. Lauren trudged wearily over and sank heavily into the passenger seat.

"I'm sorry for dragging you out," she said with a huff.

The traffic was quite heavy through Pontefract, which made progress home slow, but it eased as they headed out of town and towards Fitzwilliam. Iris picked up speed as she followed the signs to the station.

"Your grandad's finishing work a bit earlier today, so we'll all eat together," she said as they came to the station entrance. "We won't be doing that so often now will we?" she added sadly.

"London's not on the moon, Gran, and I'll be coming home lots of times," Lauren said, trying to sound brighter than she felt.

Iris said nothing and pulled up in front of Lauren's car.

"It looks like someone's left a leaflet on your windscreen," she said, noticing something wedged between the wiper blades. "I hate it when people lumber you with their junk."

Lauren shrugged. "People have to make a living," she said, clambering out of her gran's car. "Thanks for the lift, I'll see you at home."

As Iris eased slowly away, Lauren saw that what was nestled between the blades wasn't a leaflet at all but an envelope. She frowned and removed it from the wipers. It had her name written on it. She tore open the envelope, slipped out the note and read the brief message.

"Oh my God," she said in horror, covering her mouth with her hand.

Her day had just got infinitely worse.

39

The next few hours were full of turmoil. The missive had been plain enough.

By the time you read this I really will be dead. All I wanted was a chance. Sorry for all the inconvenience. Love Dad.

How Lauren had managed to drive safely home she didn't know. Perhaps the full gravity of what she'd read hadn't yet hit home, or maybe adrenaline had kicked in and done its job. How had he taken his life, an overdose? Hanged himself? What? As she sat numbed on the sofa, these questions burned in her mind like hot coals. Her phone alerted her to a fresh email, however, snapping her into the present moment. She saw it was from Kate and immediately opened it.

Phone me urgently! Her mobile number was boldly displayed

Her gran was sitting alongside her, bewildered and upset, though her sympathies were only with Lauren.

"Do you want me to call her?" she asked, unsure whether Lauren was up to the task.

Lauren shook her head and with a trembling hand, punched in the number. She engaged the speaker on her phone so her gran could hear the whole conversation. It wasn't long before Kate answered.

"Lauren?"

"Yes."

"Something terrible has happened." Kate sounded very cool. "It's about your dad…"

"I-I think I already know," Lauren said.

"How could you know?"

"There was a note on my car windscreen. Has he really… has he killed himself?"

There was a pause and the line crackled. "This afternoon at around one o'clock. He threw himself under an express train. I hope you're satisfied now."

That explained the delays on the line.

"What do you mean?"

"All he wanted was to be a part of your life and you couldn't even give him a chance." Kate almost spat the words.

Iris took the phone from Lauren as she dissolved into tears. She briefly introduced herself before leaping to Lauren's defence.

"Don't you dare blame Lauren for what's happened. If Leonard chose to take his own life it had nothing to do with anyone else. If he thought he could just talk himself back into Lauren's life—"

"Leonard is dead because he cared!" Kate cut in sharply. "He'd finally got his head straight and wanted to do the right thing by Lauren."

"People who have their head straight don't throw themselves under trains," Iris returned strongly. "The right thing for Leonard to have done was to have stayed away from Lauren altogether. The trouble and upset he's caused! My granddaughter has felt the need to move away from home completely because of that man's behaviour, and giving up a good job in the process I might add."

Kate wasn't moved. "I want to speak to Lauren; put her on."

"She's far too upset to talk."

"Upset? Well I hope she carries the guilt of what she's done for the rest of her life!"

She hung up. Iris turned immediately to Lauren who was utterly distraught.

"Don't you dare blame yourself," Iris said firmly. "The only person to blame for this… this… farce is your father."

40

Iris's words had no effect whatsoever on Lauren. The simple, unarguable fact was that her dad would still be alive had she agreed to allow him into her life. She'd suffered so many blows in recent times, but none were as hard as this and now her emotional reserves had flat-lined. The sleeping tablet her gran had given her was about as effective as a tee shirt in the arctic and as she lay on her bed staring wretchedly at the ceiling, she could find nothing within her that could lighten the lead-weighted guilt that possessed her. *"I hope she carries the guilt of what she's done for the rest of her life!"* Kate's words played in her head like a sick mantra, fusing into her brain like a parasite, and killing at source any contrary thoughts. She was beyond tears now, they'd stopped a few hours ago after her grandad had comforted her and whispered over and over that she was a good girl, and how much he and Iris loved her.

"You're a selfish little bitch." The parasite returned in Kate's voice. "Just who do you think you are? You've abandoned your boyfriend and now you've killed your dad. You killed him, Lauren. You killed him!" And so the battle went on until finally, out of sheer exhaustion, she eventually fell asleep.

41

The following week had a strange numbness to it. Surreal was an understatement. Lauren became a recluse in her room, shutting herself off from the world, alone with her dark and self-deprecating thoughts. Although she engaged with her grandparents, she was sullen and irritable with them and despite their best efforts; nothing seemed to lift her from her gloom. On Thursday afternoon there was a knock at the door and Geoff initially thought it might be the police, but when he opened the door he was surprised to see Pritvia on the doorstep. The girl looked unusually reserved, not quite the confident young lady he'd seen at Lauren's birthday party.

"I'm sorry to bother you," she said. "I've come to see Lauren if that's all right. I've been calling her phone for days, but she isn't answering. I'm really worried."

Geoff stood aside. "You'd better come in." He led her through into the living room where Iris was sewing a button onto a bright pink jacket that belonged to Lauren. She looked up.

"Hello, love. Lauren didn't say she was expecting visitors."

"I just called on the off chance I'd be able to see her."

"You've travelled a long way," Geoff said, aware that Pritvia didn't drive. Her journey must have involved at least two changes of bus.

"It's nothing," Pritvia said dismissively. "I'm not at work this week and I'd nothing else to do."

"I take it you know the ins and outs of what's happened?" Geoff said.

Pritvia nodded, glancing around for any sign of her friend.

"The only thing that travels faster than good news is bad news."

"Lauren hasn't taken it very well, she blames herself," Iris said. "She's been spending most of her time holed up in her room."

Iris went into to the hallway and yelled up the stairs.

"Lauren! Pritvia's here to see you." There was no response, which wasn't unexpected, so she went upstairs and knocked on her room door. "Lauren, did you hear me?"

A muffled grunt came from the other side.

"Do you want me to send her up or are you coming down?" Iris asked.

"I don't want to see anybody," Lauren said irritably.

"Lauren, she's travelled all the way from Leeds; I'm not sending her away."

"Why can't people just leave me alone!"

"It isn't healthy for you to be stuck in there all day, you need company, and fresh air if nothing else."

No response.

"Lauren?"

"I'll come down in a minute," Lauren growled.

"Well make sure you do."

The minute was more like five and when Lauren finally appeared she looked pale and tired. Her tee shirt hung limply from her forlorn shoulders and her jeans were as crumpled as crape paper. She forced a sheepish smile at her friend and ran a hand through her lifeless hair.

"I was really worried about you," Pritvia said, pushing her glasses onto the bridge of her nose.

"Why don't the pair of you go out for a walk or something?" Iris suggested, "or take yourselves off for something to eat. Dario's will be open; you could try there."

"Sounds cool to me," Pritvia said.

Lauren shrugged as if she'd little say in the matter.

Dario's wasn't busy which Lauren was grateful for. It was a typical pizzeria and had the luxury of spacious seating with partitions that allowed a modicum of privacy for those who wanted it. It wasn't a venue Lauren particularly frequented; despite it being just around the corner, in fact she hadn't set foot in the place since she was at school, when she'd been part of a clique of girls who'd munched pizza while trying to do homework at the same time. The results of their well-intended efforts were mediocre at best, and it hadn't taken long for their conversation to lean towards fashion, boys (in most cases) and last night's TV, as opposed to balancing equations and ploughing through history and geography assignments. The place still smelled the same as she remembered, and the staff hadn't altered much either. Lauren wasn't particularly hungry but chose the Hawaiian (ten inches with half the cheese), and Pritvia opted for the *pollo fungi* with a side helping of chips.

Lauren wasn't saying very much and was a shadow of her former self. She was picking at her pizza as if she expected it to bite her.

"How long are you going to keep screwing yourself over?" Pritvia said, having endured the discomfort of Lauren's almost zombie-like demeanour for a good twenty minutes. The girl needed a kick up the backside otherwise she'd go under.

"What?"

"I know what's happened is pretty shit, but I think you need to cut yourself some slack." The same old Pritvia, forceful and straight to the point.

"Cut myself some slack?" Lauren said indignantly. "My dad killed himself because of me. All he wanted was a chance to get to know me."

"I'm not going to apologise for being hard with you, Lauren, but I think you need to wake up and get a grip of yourself."

Lauren had no ready response to this sudden challenge and could only stare at Pritvia incredulously.

"I've been calling you for days and you never picked up once."

"Pardon me for having things on my mind," Lauren said, tetchily.

"I don't pretend to know what you're going through," Pritvia said, "but what I do know is that you can't blame yourself for what your dad has done."

"Why can't I?"

Pritvia took a breath. "Pin your ears back and listen," she said, coming across all matronly. "You told me that your dad was a stranger to you, and that you didn't want him in your life."

Lauren nodded.

Pritvia went on. "And that's exactly what you told him, right?"

Another nod.

"You didn't say that you hated him or that she should throw himself under a train."

Lauren shook her head, pushed a sliver of pizza into her mouth and chewed it slowly.

"You've done nothing wrong, Lauren. You're innocent in all of this so stop choosing to play the victim."

"I'm not playing the victim!" Lauren snapped.

"Yes, you are. I know it's a popular thing to do these days, but it doesn't wash with me. Grab your innocence, not your pain."

"That's your counselling degree talking, is it?"

Pritvia leaned forward, not to be intimidated by Lauren's irascible mood.

"Lauren, I know you don't have a mean or selfish bone in your body, and I love you for it. I also know that whatever reason you had for knocking your dad back didn't come from malice. You *know* that."

Lauren sighed and cupped her chin in her hand.

"I don't know what to think," she said. "I don't know anything any more."

"Well one thing you can be sure of," Pritvia said, still quite stern, "if you want to define yourself by what your dad did, or what Josh did, the whole of this shit that *you didn't cause*, you'll end up being totally screwed up and popping pills the rest of your life. Grab back that life of yours, Lauren and live it for Christ's sake."

Pritvia's words stayed with Lauren all night to the extent that they were all she could think about the following day. Geoff and Iris saw an improvement in her demeanour though; she hadn't shut herself in her room for one thing and had made a clear effort with her appearance. The crumpled jeans were replaced by a blue dress and her hair was freshly washed. When she said she was going into town for a mooch around, her grandparents were hopeful that at last, Lauren was finally coming out of her melancholia, no doubt thanks to Pritvia.

Her first port of call was Shakespeare's where she broke from convention and ordered a strong tea and a toasted teacake. The place wasn't busy but still retained its cosy feel and that was all she wanted. She looked at her phone, hunting for any online trivia, but her mind constantly replayed Pritvia's words. *'Grab back that life of yours, Lauren and live it for Christ's sake.'* And there was the other thing she'd said just before that, the thing that now began to lighten the pendulous clouds that still hung over her shoulders. *'If you want to define yourself by what your dad did, or what Josh did, the whole of this shit that you didn't cause, you'll end up being totally screwed up and popping pills the rest of your life.'* Define yourself. That's

212

exactly what I've been doing, Lauren thought. Defining myself by what my dad did. The realisation didn't come easily, but nevertheless, Lauren could feel something stirring within her, perhaps a sort of awakening. *If that's true for me, then it must be true of dad,* she reasoned. He'd *defined himself* by what I'd said, and he couldn't handle it. In his last selfish act on earth, he'd turned his own wretchedness onto Lauren and blamed her for his own pitiful failings. A selfish bastard to the end. As Lauren mused and reflected, she could feel a surge of anger run through her veins, it felt good. It was the fuel she would use to get her life back.

When Lauren returned home she was in reasonable spirits. However, a little later as they were all sitting relaxed over the television; Lauren snuggled up to her grandad on the sofa. It wasn't like her to be quite so clingy, as affectionate as she could be at times, but just before the news was due to start, Lauren said:

"Do you think I should go to the funeral?" It wasn't a question that either Geoff or Iris was expecting, and Lauren could feel her grandad tighten as her words registered with him.

"That's a difficult one," he said after he'd pondered over the question for a few moments. "I suppose you'll have to ask yourself what good it would do and why you want to go."

"Hmm," Lauren murmured thoughtfully.

"It could cause a lot of trouble," Iris said, all too aware of how awkward things could get. "I suppose the question is, do you *want* to go?"

Lauren gently slipped out of her grandad's arms. "I grew up thinking that Dad was dead, and now he is," she said. "After everything that's happened it would draw a line."

Iris was still circumspect. "We couldn't allow you to go on your own. We'd come with you."

"Do you think there *would* be trouble?" Lauren asked warily.

"If we keep our distance and stay at the back, we might just get away with it," Geoff said, "but let's not make any decisions now. There'll have to be an inquest first and I don't know how that affects funeral arrangements."

"And I wouldn't suppose that Kate will be passing on any information," Iris added caustically.

There were other things to think of besides the funeral. Lauren was due to go down to London on Sunday and although she said she wanted to go, she was persuaded by her grandparents to wait until after the funeral. Lauren phoned Zak and told him everything that had happened, which did her a power of good. She also told him about Pritvia's impromptu visit and the impact it had on her. The more she offloaded, the freer and less burdened she felt. Over the next few days when she was occasionally hit with a wave of guilt, she reminded herself of Pritvia's counsel and it saved her every time.

Lauren counted fourteen people at the funeral, and that included herself and her grandparents. They sat right on the back row of the chapel, leaving a gap of at least eight rows between themselves and the rest of the gathering. Kate had seen them as they'd arrived and wasted no time in shooting Lauren an incriminatory look that could have turned water to ice in seconds. Lauren had immediately averted her gaze and kept her head bowed throughout the service. The minister did her best to paint a decent picture of Leonard, hiding his sins behind a wall of mental health issues that the man had battled bravely to the end. His suicide was described as a tragedy born of rejection that perhaps a softer heart might have averted. These words were a devastating blow, and they took Lauren and her grandparents completely by surprise. Geoff put a consoling arm around Lauren as she sobbed heavily, stroking her hair, kissing her forehead, soothing... ever soothing...

But Lauren was not destroyed. She knew in her heart that she hadn't rejected her dad out of vengeance or hatred; he simply didn't fit in with her plans for the future and never had done. He was the one who had jumped to the conclusion that she was giving him hope when she'd pushed for them to meet, not her, and he was the one who couldn't face that fact. All Lauren had ever wanted from him was answers. It's not my fault! she told herself as she dried away her tears. He did this to himself.

When the service ended, and the guests filed out, Geoff and Iris wanted to sneak out unseen, but Lauren flatly refused.

"No," she said with grim determination. "I'm going to walk right past Kate and look her in the eye."

"Lauren, no," Iris said. "It isn't appropriate."

"I've done my duty today," Lauren said, "and I'm having my life back. She blames me for Dad's death and I'm not having it. You can come with me or go to the car."

"Geoff, can't you stop her?"

He was looking at Lauren almost reverently.

"No," he said, moved by her bravery. "I'm right with you Lauren… what about you Iris?"

Iris took a breath and closed her eyes. "All right!" she said. "Let's just get it over with."

They linked arms as they filed out of the chamber. Kate was outside now, shaking hands with friends and relatives, stoically accepting their condolences. As she saw Lauren and her grandparents' approach, her face turned to granite. Lauren broke forward and drew close to her. Although Lauren's eyes were red and moist, she locked them straight into Kate's hard glare.

"I don't know how you *dare* show your face," Kate hissed.

Lauren took a moment to compose herself. "I didn't promise him a thing," she said.

"All your dad wanted was to make things right with you and you threw him away like he was a piece of rubbish."

"No, *he* thought he was a piece of rubbish, not me," Lauren said pointedly. "He had a life with you, and he should have left it at that. I didn't ask him to start following me."

"You're a cold-hearted bitch."

"That's the only thing you've said I wish was true."

Geoff tugged on Lauren's arm. "Come on, love, time to go."

The next few days passed slowly, allowing Lauren to concentrate on packing her things for London. When the day of her departure arrived it had a surreal feel to it, even the train was bang on time, a lucky omen perhaps.

"This is it," Lauren said as the train slowed and finally came to a halt in front of her. "Next stop London!"

Geoff and Iris put on brave faces for Lauren's sake.

"Do you need help with your case?" Geoff asked as Lauren extended the handle.

"It's not too heavy," she said, "I can manage."

They all embraced.

"You might want to check your bank balance when you get the chance," Geoff said easing himself away.

Lauren frowned. She noticed a twinkle in her grandad's eye that suggested there was nothing to worry about.

"You will phone won't you?" Iris said tightly.

"Don't fuss, Gran," Lauren said.

Iris embraced Lauren again and kissed her on the cheek. "Say hello to Zak for me."

"Of course."

"And let us know what you want to do about your car," Geoff said. "Once you know the lay of the land we can bring it down for you if that's what you want."

"I will."

She got on the train and waved at them through the window. Geoff was miming and mouthing, "Phone!" at her. "Look at your phone!"

"What?" she mimed back.

Geoff went up to the window and said slowly, "Check your bank, on your phone…"

The train started to pull away, Geoff stepped back. Lauren opened up her banking app. Her eyes widened and she was forced to take a breath, covering her wide-open mouth with her hand. She saw that her balance had been boosted by five thousand pounds. She bit down hard on her lip, clearly moved by the gesture and immediately called her grandad. He was quick to respond.

"Thank you," Lauren said, "you didn't need to do that. It's such a lot of money."

"You're worth every penny, sweetheart," Geoff said warmly. "It might help out a bit, eh? Go and make London sing your song, Lauren."

"I will. I love you, Grandad."

"I love you too, Lauren."

42

Her first day in London as an official resident was a bit of a haze, but as she unpacked and made the spare room her own, she was filled with a quiet assurance that she'd made the right decision. In the evening, lazing on the sofa, she gazed out over the London skyline, feeling a warm glow in her stomach. The brave new world was waiting for her. Zak came in from the kitchen and eased himself beside her, handing her a glass of merlot.

"To exciting times," he said, grinning that boyish grin of his.

"To exciting times," Lauren beamed. Zak placed an affectionate arm around Lauren, and she rested her head on his shoulder. She closed her eyes and gave a soft purr.

"Thanks for everything, Zak," she said. "I really appreciate what you're doing for me."

"That's what friends are for isn't it?"

Lauren snuggled into him. "How come you don't have a girlfriend?"

Zak laughed self-consciously, "I don't know. Maybe I'm not tall enough."

Lauren frowned in amusement. "That's silly talk."

Zak didn't say anything and began stroking Lauren's hair. She looked up at him, her large eyes full of warmth.

"You can kiss me if you want to," she said, reddening a little.

Zak smiled and pressed his lips gently against hers. He could taste the merlot on her lips as she responded with a passion that surprised him.

When they eventually drew apart he said, "I should have done that a long time ago."

"Yes," Lauren said. "You should have done."

As Lauren's world began to expand with the prospect of ever widening horizons, so Josh's world closed in on him and threatened to shut him out altogether. The realities of prison life, perpetually having to watch your back, stay vigilant and ensure you stayed on the right side of the inmates you needed to were taking their toll. The only chink of hope to bring some light into his day was the prospect of hearing from Lauren. He was desperate to see her again though, he longed for her so much that his stomach ached every time he thought of her. But any communication was better than nothing, so when he was informed he had mail, his heart skipped somersaults.

Josh knew the letter was from Lauren before the wing officer handed him the envelope. He recognised her neat, large handwriting. He noticed that it had a London postmark and it had been posted several days ago. The officer waited for him to open it. Those were the rules. The officer didn't need to read the letter, it was to make sure there was nothing smuggled inside the envelope. Not that there would ever have been a chance of that happening with Lauren. Once the officer was satisfied that everything was fine, Josh was free to go on his way. He went back to his cell, realising he was shaking. What she might have to say meant so much to him. She was his life after all. He pushed the envelope to his nose, trying to detect any trace of perfume that might be lingering there and then slipped the letter out of the envelope. He took some breaths before he read the first line.

Dear Josh,

I hope you are doing okay as far as okay can ever be when you aren't free. I know it can't be easy for you, and I truly am sorry for everything that has happened. Yes, I do feel guilty, maybe I'll never forgive myself for not going to the police when you said I should and all this could have been avoided, however, things were complicated as you now know. But you do have anger issues, regardless of what happened, and those issues aren't fun to live with. I know you have a tender side and that deep down you want to give and receive love, who doesn't? But I want to make it clear that there can be no future for us. I want to put everything behind me and start afresh. You can too. I think a lot of your anger issues come from your poor relationship with your mum and dad and I am sure you can get help for that, counselling perhaps? I know that you love me, but this isn't a letter of hope, Josh. You must understand that. I'm just a normal girl, I want normal things. I don't want a volatile partner, or to be worried that the least little thing might cause you to kick off. If you love me as you say you do, please let me go and don't write back or think that we can have a second chance. I don't want that. All I can do is offer you my sincere best wishes, I truly hope you can fix things with your parents and after the nightmare is over for you, to find a life that is filled with happiness. I'm very sorry.

Lauren x

He was angry when he'd finished reading. How cold-hearted could she be! Everything they'd been through together, dismissed in just a few lines. He wanted to tear the letter to shreds and scatter it to the ground like confetti, stamp on it, burn it even, but as his hands were poised to rip the letter apart, he found that he couldn't do it. It was all he had of her. He read the letter again, then again, over and over until it burned into his mind. No hope, she was telling him. Fresh start. Who the hell did she think she was! *You're the reason I'm in here,* he lamented with bitter anger. *Fuck you! Fuck you!* He thumped the wall until his knuckles bled. *Fuck you, Lauren.* He got off his bunk and went to the far side of the cell where a calendar marking the days to his release was attached. His eyes fell on June 9th, 2026, and stared at it, his rage and impatience on the verge of making him explode. He daubed the date with his blood.